THE
ROBERT OLEN BUTLER
PRIZE STORIES 2009

*

THE
ROBERT OLEN BUTLER
PRIZE STORIES 2009

*

— DEL SOL PRESS • WASHINGTON D. C. —

CONTENTS

THE POSSIBILITY OF THINGS

ANNIE WEATHERWAX

Today is January 10, my sixteenth birthday, and all I want is an iPod.

"We'll be lucky if we can afford cake," my mother had yelled, cradling the phone to her ear. She is always on the phone and always yelling, mostly at the insurance company trying to get some kind of treatment—"Not even experimental!"—for my brother, Tommy. My parents had mortgaged and re-mortgaged everything to pay for what the insurance didn't. So now, I'm sure, when I meet them later, all I will probably get is cake.

My best friend Nita is taking me to the new Wal-Mart Supercenter in Thompson to check out the iPods anyway.

"They're cheaper there," Nita says, as I get into her car. Everyone I know has an iPod; Nita is the only one I know who has two. "They get their stuff discount from the Chinese and then they hire homeless people and retards to sell it," she says.

"Cool," I say, and we speed off.

The car she drives is her own. A Cadillac V8 Luxury, one step up from the V6 her grandparents drive. Wide and confident, it makes me feel safe, and I let myself think that somehow, I will get an iPod.

Even though the only thing she has ever bought me was chips, I tell myself, it's my birthday, and maybe this time will be different. Maybe Nita will buy me an iPod. Or I'll buy it myself, even though all I ever have in my pocket is five dollars. That is the thing about a car. It can make you feel bigger than you really are.

We head north on Route 6. The winter sun is setting fast. Clouds are taking its place. It's freezing, but all I'm wearing is a sweatshirt. I lost my jacket weeks ago and nobody cares because Tommy's back in the hospital—this time they took out his lung. But I hardly feel the cold anymore, because my best times now are when he's gone and my parents are away, always at the hospital with him. Now, I can drive around with Nita, stick my head out the window and feel the wind, cool and fast on my face, and my parents hardly notice I'm gone.

"What you really need is your own crisis," Nita says, as I pull my head back in the car.

What she means by "my own crisis," I am not sure, but I consider it seriously, because Nita is like the Dalai Lama to me. She can buy anything. She got rich from a settlement when her parents were killed in a freak accident at Home Depot. They were looking at nuts or bolts or something when an avalanche of Shop Vacs fell on them. An "avalanche." That's how Nita said it was described in the lawsuit. Apparently, the whole shelving system fell on them and when they pulled everything off, there was a DeWalt table saw in with the Shop Vacs, and this, according to the autopsy, was what killed them.

So, at age twelve, Nita moved up from Texas to live with her grandparents, and even though she still wears cowboy boots and talks with a twang, nobody makes fun of her, because she's already made something of herself. She's the Home Depot Orphan and everyone knows it.

"The best kind of crisis," Nita says, rounding the corner with one hand, palm open on the steering wheel, "is the kind that makes people feel sorry for you and makes you rich at the same time." She takes a bite out of her fingernail, rolls the window down a crack and spits it out. "Or," she says, "the other kind of crisis is the self-imposed one, you know, like the starvation diet."

Route 6 is one big strip mall and we are at a standstill, sitting in traffic. The wind swirls around us, holding its breath for a minute then letting it out, spitting pebbles and road dust against the car. Out my window a woman in high heels and bleached hair is pumping gas at a Mobil Station. The wind picks up a piece of garbage; a flattened out paper cup rises up off the pavement and hits her in the face. She brushes it away casually, like a strand of hair, as if she's used to things flying up and hitting her.

"There's always suicide," I say, still looking at the woman.

Along with gastric bypass surgery and sex change operations, suicide is our favorite topic and we discuss it whenever we get the chance. I would do it in the car with the garage door closed because, first of all, you could listen to the radio and, second of all, there wouldn't be blood to mess up your outfit. Nita would take her car with her. "I'd ride off the Brooklyn Bridge." She tilts her head towards the sky as if she's sailing through it right now. However we decide to do it, we both agree to blame Judy Pratt in our suicide notes. We don't even really know her; we just hate her. She's popular and doesn't talk to us. We discuss all this and then, like we are both seriously considering it, we stare out the window in opposite directions.

"It's too bad you can't just get your own disease," Nita finally says, as the traffic in front of us moves forward.

"Yeah," I say, "whatever," and we drive off.

The only thing I ever saw die was a squirrel. I was nine, Tommy was thirteen, and it was mid-July. He was dribbling his basketball on the driveway, I was eating a peanut butter sandwich, and the squirrel was sitting up on his haunches twitching his nose in my direction. So I tore off a piece and threw it to him. He ran forward, grabbed it in his mouth, then zigzagging, guarding it like a football, he darted toward the street for the woods. He was running fast, but then he stopped, stunned by what was heading towards him. Brakes screeched, a car swerved, the driver slowed down. He looked in the rearview mirror for a second and drove off, leaving the squirrel—his back legs flattened to the road, he clawed at the pavement with his front, desperate to get up and finish his journey to the other side.

My father ran out of the house and grabbed the shovel. He was a high school math teacher. He calculated everything carefully. This was the only time I'd seen him do anything without thinking about it first. He ran over to the squirrel, and, with one whack, he finished the job. "Sometimes, you've just got to put a thing out of its misery," he said, as he scooped it up. Tying the handles of a plastic Stop and Shop bag, he threw the squirrel away in the trash.

"Nita," I say. "What do you think they did with my brother's lung?"

"I don't know," she says, "they probably just threw it out or something."

"You mean, like in a plastic bag?"

"Yeah, either that or they just flushed it down the toilet."

We are at a stop light and it's beginning to rain. A slow old man passes by in our headlights. He is hunched over, wearing a bright yellow rain jacket. He opens his umbrella and braces it against the wind.

The light turns green. Nita steps on the gas.

"Sometimes I wish he'd just die already," I say.

I look over at Nita. Beyond her, out the window, neon signs whiz by in the dark—red, yellow, blue, green, smearing together like finger paints on a wall. The only thing not moving is Nita, small and anchored to her seat.

"Yeah," she says, "I know."

My mother had done everything; she'd tried herbs and acupuncture, she'd been to Boston and Berkeley, talked to doctors and researchers, looking for a way to save my brother.

Just this week she staged her own one-person sit-in when she went to the insurance company's downtown office and sat in the waiting room overnight, refusing to leave until somebody talked to her. But in the morning, the police came to our house and my father had to go get her.

For a while, when she got home, she sputtered around the kitchen, tired and disoriented like a moth on the ground with a broken wing. "If this was the sixties," she finally said, "there would have been a hundred of us." But it wasn't the sixties, it was 2008. So she just collapsed into the overstuffed chair in the family room and stayed there, waiting, it seemed, for it to swallow her up. She held her face in her hand. My father had left for the hospital and I was on my way out. I waited for her to look up, but she didn't move. She sat there formless and vague—a heap in the chair I no longer recognized. I hardly knew her anymore. She had become generic—the mother whose kid had cancer and that was it, as if there was nothing more to know about her. Not the fact that she'd met Gloria Steinem once and had a picture to prove it, or the fact that she went to high school with Sting. My brother's cancer had become the only thing about her.

"Are you okay?" I finally asked. And she half raised her hand, and then let it flop back down. It was all she could do; raise that one hand and let it fall, but it was the best conversation we'd had in weeks.

The automatic door opens and closes behind us. A blast of white light blinds me. My eyes slowly focus. I am vaguely aware of music lulling me from above—"Yesterday," by the Beatles, elaborately plucked out on a harp.

"Wow," I say. Nita and I are finally at Wal-Mart.

"See what I was saying?" We whisper like we are in church.

"This is amazing," I say. I have never been to a Wal-Mart Super-center before.

"They're even bigger in Texas," Nita says.

It is massive. One of everything in the world might be right here.

We just stand there looking, not knowing which way to go. And then, with no apparent direction, we begin to move.

We wander around trying to find what we are looking for. But we get distracted. There are so many things we want, that we forget why we came.

"Whoa," Nita says, "look at this one. It speaks." She is holding an electric toothbrush in a giant plastic package.

"Really?" I say.

"Yeah, look. It's an 'indicator' brush. It tells you when to stop brushing and then, when you need to go out and buy a new one."

"Cool," I say.

"Everything has indicators now. It's a good trend. People just don't know anymore what they're supposed to do," she says.

"And now," I say, "you don't even have to brush. All you have to do is hold it up to your face."

For a minute we both hold onto the package and look at the toothbrush, trapped and gleaming, staring out at us behind its bulbous plastic housing. I need one of these, we both say. And for a while we are lost in the possibility of this thing—what it might do for us and how it might change our lives.

And then, like all of a sudden, we hate it, we drop it. "Let's go," Nita says, and we leave it on the shelf.

We wander around like that, stopping and holding things, rotating them in our hands and then dropping them. Time passes, and it is hard to tell how much.

I am not sure how we get there, but we find the TVs; hundreds of them, giant and flat. People are staring up at them with their mouths open. All tuned to the same program, Who Wants to be a Millionaire? blares out at us. It's tense, this show. Laser lights flash and all they want to know for two thousand dollars from the skinny little bald man is which product is not a cereal: Fruity Freakies, Alphabits, Life or Twinkies? And when he says, "Life, final answer, because life is what you live," we all groan. Shaking our heads, we turn to go and realize the entire time we were staring at the TVs, the iPods were right behind us.

"Explain to me about this iPod," my father had said. So I told him what I knew. "Imagine that," he said. I knew he couldn't give me one, but to have him listen, to see his eyes widen as I spoke, was almost good enough. Standing here looking at them now, I wish he was next to me, so I could show him.

The Classic, the Shuffle, the Nano, the Touch iPod, are all here. Bolted down to their carpeted display, they are lined up like a family portrait. I touch them all, circling my finger around the middle wheel and pressing the center button.

"You have to get an iPod," Nita says, and the way she says it, I know she's right. More that anything I need an iPod.

"This is the one you should get," Nita says. "It holds like fifty billion songs." "Wow," I say, staring at it.

We both touch the smooth black surface of it. It is elegant and simple. I stroke it, gently, the way you might pet a caterpillar, half expecting it to come alive and speak.

"You like it?" she says, the way an aunt or an uncle might say when they're about to buy you something.

"Yeah," I say, breathless.

She sighs, like she's thinking about it. But then she looks up, "Hey," she says, tugging my arm so I'm facing her. "How about I go buy us some Doritos? I'm dying for some, aren't you? I'll go get us some and meet you back at the car."

"Whatever," I say, and she leaves. Doritos. I don't even like them.

I stand there and I tell myself I'm glad she's gone. I look back at the iPods. I don't care how I get one, I need one, so I start pulling. I tug at one, hoping it will come off. I want to hold it. I want to gather them all up and take them home. I want to hug them. I want to be an iPod. But then, someone coughs. It is a small weak cough, but I am devastated by it. I look up and see, at the end of the aisle, a woman in a wheelchair. And then I remember it's my birthday because I remember the cancer and the cake at the hospital and I am supposed to meet them there to eat it.

My brother was running. That was all he was doing: running. And then he fell. I saw him because he ran by me. It was an ordinary day in October almost three years ago. I remembered the back of him, watching his arms pump the air. I remembered the way the wind tussled his brown hair and rippled the fabric of his shirt—gently, respectful of the visible muscle underneath. He had grown a lot that year. He had started to shave. And then, he fell. Just dropped to the ground. There was no stumble or trip. It was an unnatural crashing, the way a bird gets shot out of the sky.

The woman in the wheelchair looks at me, and I realize she is not a woman, but a girl. Her eyes are brown with flecks of yellow—distant and small behind her glasses like children at the end of a tunnel. Her head is bent, resting on one shoulder hunched in a permanent shrug. She's wearing a Wal-Mart tag and I can see her name is Eve. She curls her thin lip and smiles at me, or maybe she glares. These days I cannot tell the difference, but whatever she does, it makes me feel bad for just standing up in front of her.

I remember my brother's x-ray. The fracture in his leg and the doctor's red marker circling the lesions on his bone like destination points on a map, and then, the girl turns. Soundlessly, like a snake, she wheels by.

All of a sudden, I hate being here. I hate Wal-Mart. I am left standing there feeling bad about my bones. I have never broken one. I have never even twisted an ankle, but I am always waiting. I am waiting now to fall. I hold onto the display and for a minute, I can almost feel my own bones cracking underneath me.

But then, I notice the cabinet below is open. There is an iPod, a Nano, the coolest of them all, just sitting there. The box, with its shiny silver apple and one forbidden bite, stares up at me. I could just take it. All I'd have to do is reach out and grab it. I pick my foot up off the floor and give the box a little kick. It moves. Nothing is bolted down or broken; not the bones of my legs or the iPod.

I bend down. I pull up on my sock. I untie and retie my sneaker. I stick my hand in the cabinet and touch it, and when I turn it over, I realize the security tag is gone. All that remains of it is a white scar on the black box where it used to be. It is then that I decide that this one is mine. I reach out and in the cradle of my arms, I tuck it under my sweatshirt and take it. Life: it can be so easy.

"Want some?" Nita shouts over the radio when I get in the car. On her way to the Doritos she must have forgotten about them, because what she ended up with are Cheez-its.

"Sure," I say, and grab one.

"What'd you get?" she asks.

"An iPod," I say, stretching my legs out and leaning back.

"No, really, what you get? Gum or something?" She leans forward looking for a bag.

"What? You don't believe me?" I say.

"Well, where is it?"

I pull it out and in the darkened car it appears out of my sweat-shirt as if it came from inside me.

"Whoa," she says, turning down the radio. "A Nano," she takes it and holds it in front of her. "I could have gotten one of these." She bites her fingernail fast and loud and I can tell she's jealous because Nita doesn't own a Nano. She turns it over in her hands and when she's done she hands it back to me fast. She starts the car, flicks on the wipers, shifts it into reverse and pulls out.

"Hey, wait a minute," she says, before she drives forward, "where'd you get the money?"

"What? You think you're the only one with money," I say.

"Hmmm," she says, and looks at me like she's seeing me for the first time. "Cool." She raises her eyebrows, and nods her head. It is pouring out now, and the wind blows shivers through the park-ing lot puddles. She shifts the car into drive, and it moves forward through the rain like it's nothing.

Nita drops me off at the hospital and gives me the Wal-Mart bag with what's left of the Cheez-its. I put the iPod in the bag, stick a Cheez-it in my mouth and watch her pull away. I realize that she doesn't know it, but she is too small for that car. She strains to see over the dashboard. The further she gets the smaller she becomes, so that it looks as if the car is driving itself until it rounds the corner and is gone.

I stand in front of the hospital and look up at the bit of sky visible between the buildings. The rain has turned to snow. The wind catch-es it, swirling it in the light, making it seem as if it is falling up.

I step forward and another set of automatic doors opens up in front of me. I walk the familiar white hall. I try not to look up or inside the rooms, or at anyone who passes me, afraid I might see something in them I know. I hear the squeaking of rubber sole shoes on the hospital floor. I pass a bucket and mop squealing as someone wheels it by. I go left at the receptionist desk, right at the gift shop, up at the second set of elevators and off at the eighth floor. People die here. They either get better and go home or they die.

"Don't you think we should bury it?" I asked my brother about the squirrel. It was the day after it got hit and every time I saw a living one, I thought about the dead one lying in our trash and how it was my peanut butter sandwich that set it heading for the woods in the first place.

"What for?" Tommy said. He had his bike turned upside down on the driveway and was spinning the wheels.

"I don't know. What if it has a mother or something?"

"Squirrels don't have mothers," he said. These days, he'd say anything to get rid of me.

"What if it does?" I said.

"I told you. They don't, they only have themselves."

He kept spinning the wheels on his bike and I kept watching him.

"Why are you just standing there?" he said.

"I don't know," I said.

He stood up, rolled his eyes, grabbed the shovel, fetched the squirrel in the bag out of the trash and headed for the woods.

"Well," he said, "don't just stand there. Come on."

I followed my brother into the woods along the creek behind our house until he got to a spot and stopped.

"Here okay?" he said, stabbing the shovel into the earth.

I looked around. "Back further," I said.

He rolled his eyes again, but moved his shovel back to where I was standing. He dug a hole and, laying the bag gently down, he buried the squirrel.

"There," he said, giving the earth one last pat with the back of the shovel before he stood up and turned to go.

"Aren't you going to say anything?" I asked.

"Like what?"

"I don't know. I just think we're supposed to say something is all."

He sighed. "Come on," he said, gesturing with his head, "come over here." He grabbed my shoulder and drew me into him. He bent his head toward earth, closed his eyes and I did the same.

"Dear God," my brother said, "please send this squirrel to heaven so my sister will stop bugging me."

It wasn't exactly what I was hoping for. I opened one eye and looked up at him, waiting for him to say something more. His eyes were still closed. I felt his arm around my shoulder. The wind hushed the trees and scattered sunlight across his face. A bead of sweat hesitated, and then rolled down the side of his cheek. He never stood still anymore. He was always going somewhere or doing something, so when a fly landed on my forehead, I didn't move. In the sticky summer heat, crickets and peepers sang. An owl hooted in the distance and the fly walked across the bridge of my nose and left of its own accord. My brother opened his eyes.

"Feel better?" he asked.

"Yeah," I said, and I did.

It was the only funeral I had ever been to, but when I walk into room 802 and look up, I know this time, he might die here. He is small and gray in his hospital bed. He has a needle up his arm that goes to a bag by his side. A machine hooked to his heart beeps, beeps, beeps a rhythm behind the sucking sound of air flowing in, and out, from the tank to the tubes up his nose.

My parents are there too, like they always are. My mother on one side in jeans and a sweater, my father on the other side in a tie, sleeves rolled up half way. My mother has folded my brother's bathrobe. She's organized the magazines on the table next to him. There are flowers, long past being fresh, but she has filled the vase with new water anyway, and it reminds me of home, of her, and how she used to be before all this happened.

The only thing that is different is the cake. Not even a whole one, but pieces on Styrofoam plates sitting on a hospital tray. One slice is knocked over on its side, the layer of white frosting at the point peeling back slightly and I know this one is mine. The candle, dislodged from its hole by its collapse, lies next to it.

My brother's eyes move slowly and he notices the bag in my hand.

With each word he takes a full breath. "What'd—you—get?" he asks.

I look down at the bag forgetting for a minute that I had it.

"Cheez-its," I say a little too loudly, "want some?" and I reach in, grab the box, and hold it out to him.

His whole chest moves upward underneath the blanket, like he's about to say something, but then he pukes. His spit up is green this time. I've seen it when it was black, but this time there is color. Bright. Too bright. It shines almost, against the dull grey-white of his skin and the hospital sheets and the whole room.

My mother glares at me. "Put those away," she says.

"We'll have some later, kiddo," my father says. Nobody notices, but my father confuses me with my brother because he reaches out and musses up my hair the way he only used to with Tommy.

I stand there and stare at the floor. I am afraid to look up. I am afraid to see my mother wiping my brother's face.

Maybe it's because I feel bad, maybe it's because I don't know what else to do, but I reach into the Wal-Mart bag and give him the iPod.

"Here. And this, I got this for you."

My mother steps back. He glances up. "Wow," he says, and I place it in front of him on his stomach.

"Would you look at that," my father says.

My mother grabs my arm and pulls me aside. "Where'd you get that?" she says.

But I don't answer. I don't even look at her.

"Look at me," she squeezes my arm—a hidden slap. "Look at me," she yells in a whisper.

Finally, I raise my eyes and from behind my bangs I meet her gaze.

"Answer me," she says.

"Wal-Mart," I say. "They were cheaper there."

She looks back at me and more than anything I want to look away, but as if in a dare, I keep my eyes fixed on hers.

"I should make you bring that back right now," she says.

Make me, I want to say, but I don't have to. She looks at me with watery eyes, not because she is about to cry, but because, I can tell, she is tired. She is exhausted. Her grip on me loosens. And I realize then, that if my mother could steal what she wanted, she would. If it was there and she could take it, without a thought, she'd grab it. So she drops her gaze. She sighs. She lets go of my arm and touches my forehead. She brushes back my bangs the way she used to.

"Jesus," she says. "Let's just hope nobody saw you."

The fluorescent overhead hospital light shimmers and makes it seem as if we are moving, as if we could be falling and I remember hearing somewhere, that when a bird gets shot, it is not the bullet, but the fall to earth that kills it. But we are not falling. We are standing still looking at the iPod, swaddled in the blankets of my brother's hospital bed. As if it might hold the possibility of life, we wait.

THE FINALISTS

THE APPRAISAL

JACOB M. APPEL

"Sixty-three," said Abbie. "It *feels* like only half a life."

She stood at the open window and gazed through the bars. Outside, the city pulsed in its usual frenzy. A street merchant had spread his wares on the sidewalk in front of the school—books, records, baseball memorabilia. Across Riverside Drive, a dark-skinned nanny wheeled two light-skinned babies in a perambulator. Farther down the block, an elderly Chinese couple was shaking the branches of the ginko trees. They did this every June, collecting bucketfuls of the soft, stinking fruit. Abbie wondered what they did with the fruit, but she'd never gotten around to asking.

"They're making progress every day," said Bert. "All sorts of advances."

Abbie turned to face him. "It's funny. I can remember when anything past sixty seemed absolutely ancient." She surveyed the bare classroom. In one corner stood the boxes of picture books and art supplies that belonged to St. Mary's. Two smaller cartons, marked PERSONAL, would go home with her. "Did you know that when my grandmother turned eighty, she received a framed certificate from President Truman?"

"You can fight this," said Bert. "Don't croak on one doctor's opinion."

"To what end? To die like Leonard?" asked Abbie. "I won't go through that."

She'd married Leonard shortly after Bert had divorced her. (Sometimes she quipped she'd lost one husband to another man, the other to another world.) Leonard's final months in the chronic care facility—she called it the *gulag*—had been wretched. He'd suffered a series of small strokes. Each carried off a piece of him—as water smoothes sand.

"Is there anything I can say?" asked Bert. He was sitting on her desk, his short legs dangling over the side. Much of his hair was long gone. The orange tufts at the corners of his scalp resembled giant earmuffs. "What haven't I thought of?"

"I asked *you* that, once," answered Abbie. "Remember?" That had been the morning he'd revealed his relationship with Wesley, an episode now almost inaccessibly remote. She crossed the room and settled beside him on the desktop. For the first time in thirty years, she took his hand in hers. "It's too late to say anything," she said. "I know what death's about. And I'm not afraid of it, not terribly. But to end up alone in a sterile white room with a handful of meager possessions—*that* scares the living shit out of me."

Bert nodded, polishing his forehead with his fingers.

"I've thought everything through," continued Abbie. "Having a tumor in your lung makes your mind work overtime." She liked to imagine the growth as solid but delicate like the heart of a songbird. That, of course, had been months ago—before the diagnosis, before the cancer slithered into her bones. "I haven't led the life I wanted," Abbie said.

"You've taught all these children."

"But I didn't change them. Not the way some teachers do." For years she'd labored at it, but teaching wasn't her gift. Her wit confused the children. Eventually, she'd given up trying. "It was a waste. I want my death to have meaning," she said. "Like the heroes I teach the children about. Like Joan of Arc and Anne Hutchinson and Nathan Hale declaring, 'I regret that I have but one life to give for me country.'"

"To raise awareness," agreed Bert.

Abbie squeezed his hand. "In a way. Please don't think I'm crazy, Bert, but I'm going to set myself on fire."

Bert said nothing, at first. Abbie stared down at her toes, then across the room at the globe and the filing cabinet. Under the American flag, the oscillating fan whirled with silent grace.

"To protest the war. Like during Vietnam," Abbie explained. "I know I've led a mediocre life. I'm not a fool. But what's that quote from Ralph Waldo Emerson? *Consistency is the hobgoblin of little minds*. Well, I'm going to do something inconsistent for a change. Something *grand*. I may have lived a mediocre life—at best—but I'm not going to die a mediocre death."

"You're serious?"

"Dead serious," she answered. "That's why I called you."

"You can't do this," said Bert.

"I can do this. I *will* do this. And I need your help."

The idea had come to Abbie at the beauty salon.

Usually, she had her hair done around the corner. Her stylist, Vin, was a no-nonsense gay kid from the streets of Baltimore. He worked quickly. He had steady hands you could trust not to lop your ears off. Both of his grandfathers had been barbers back in Sicily. She'd always thought his shop cozy, a blend of Old Neighborhood and Old World, but now, with the claw of death reaching for her across the horizon, it struck her as drab. *So much* of her past, her present, suddenly seemed drab—as though she'd lived, unknowingly, to the wattage of a low-energy bulb. Maybe that was why, on the morning after her diagnosis, Abbie walked past Vin's window and crossed Amsterdam Avenue to the glitzy salon that had replaced the Filipino laundromat. She'd craved change. She wanted to spend money frivolously.

All of the furniture in the new salon was black and angular. The women waiting ahead of her were half her age. Abbie sat down. She pulled *The Forsyte Saga* from her canvas bag. The book seemed excessively long. Was it worth the investment? It might be the last book she'd ever read. The girl in the next chair, a bleached blonde with an eyebrow ring, was reading *Beyond the Perfect Orgasm*. Maybe that was a better choice. Or possibly Proust. Unable to concentrate, Abbie folded shut her novel. A conversation between two of the stylists caught her attention, though several seconds elapsed as she laced together its threads.

"But would you do it?" asked the stylist nearest the window. She was a sharp-featured young woman who reminded Abbie of an angry pigeon. "I mean if there were no personal consequences. If you could walk away scot-free."

"Fuck, Summer," said her male coworker. He was tall and emaciated—what Abbie called *concentration camp chic*. His voice rolled in waves. "Where do you think up these questions?"

"They just come to me," said Summer.

Summer snipped at the bangs of an unsmiling brunette, cutting more empty space than hair. Her work struck Abbie as impersonal. Like getting trimmed by a topiary gardener.

"Think about all the suffering he's caused," Summer persisted. "You would have killed Hitler, wouldn't you?"

"Jesus Christ," said her co-worker. "I don't know."

It suddenly registered with Abbie: These kids were talking about assassinating the President. Abstractly, of course. But none-the-less a statement about the plight of the world, about the lunatics she would no longer live to see destroy it. This was the second time she'd overheard strangers discussing the President's death. The previous week, she'd had dinner with a retired colleague. The couple at the next table, clearly on a first date, were debating the appropriate response to learning that the madman in the Oval Office had been shot. *He'd* said glee. *She'd* insisted upon relief. Halfway through the meal, they were kissing. Meanwhile, Abbie's companion lamented a world gone to hell in a hand basket. "When JFK died," he'd said, "I lost a brother."

When Kennedy was shot, Abbie had been younger than the stylist.

"I'd do it," said Summer. "I really would."

Her coworker signaled for the next woman in line. "So it's settled," he said.

The brunette rose from Summer's chair. She was closer to Abbie's age than the stylist's, attractive, though the skin of her face looked too tight. "I don't think you should kill anybody," she interjected. "Ever." Her voice held a deep sadness. "If you're upset with things—and there's certainly enough to be upset about—you should put yourself on the line. Like Gandhi or Martin Luther King."

"I guess so," agreed Summer.

The brunette stepped around Summer. Abbie assumed her place in the chair. When the woman had paid and departed, the male stylist said: "Way to upset the customers."

"Screw you," said Summer. "I'm still right." She scooped up Abbie's hair in her bony hand. "What are we going to do today?"

"Not much," said Abbie. "I want to look like Grace Kelly."

The stylist smiled blankly. Abbie felt old and useless.

"Just a joke," she said. "Whatever you sense works best."

Already, though, she was thinking about putting herself on the line. She'd never done anything *particularly* political before, but the need had never seemed so great. Besides, it would help make up for frittering her life away. That, after all, was what she'd done. She'd never opened up that catering company, never gone back for her doctorate. Instead, she'd passed her days keeping things in their place (And there'd been so many minor crises, dripping knapsacks, bruised elbows, valises left on airplanes—). And now Leonard was dead. Her parents were dead. Her son, Norman, was as good as dead—she hadn't spoken to him in a decade. (The boy hadn't even come to his father's funeral.) For years it had torn her apart, had nearly torn her marriage apart. She'd tried visiting him once, in prison, when he served time for passing bad checks. He'd have none of it. Another of her failures. Thinking about Norman made Abbie miserable, so she no longer did.

Summer massaged shampoo into her scalp. "Do you think you'd like some color? Maybe a hint of vermilion?"

"Yes," said Abbie. "Whatever."

She was recalling the first time she'd seen Leonard teach. He'd been a bioethics professor at Columbia. "Do you know what this is?" he asked, holding up a strand of rope. He paced the lecture hall, sweat beading at his temples. "Not any old string," he declaimed.

"Not your run-of-the-mill, butcher's block string. No, no, Nanette! This is my *lucky* piece of string." Here Leonard had paused, leaning forward over his lectern. The veins bulged above his temples. Perspiration glistened at the end of his nose. "If you intentionally destroy my lucky piece of string," he demanded, "to how much compensation am I entitled?" And then he'd asked about human life: What was it worth? How was "Grandma"—unemployable, of limited social use—any more valuable than his lucky piece of string? Abbie's first husband, Bert, was an appraiser of artwork and collectibles. But Leonard—Leonard had been an *appraiser of lives*.

"Maybe you should kill yourself," said Abbie.

The stylist was still kneading Abbie's head. "What, honey?"

"Self-immolation. Don't kill the President. Kill yourself in protest."

As she said the words, they struck Abbie as surprisingly convincing. Later—when she shared her plans with Bert—she would realize how much easier it was to make the decision than to explain it. She'd compared it to coming up with the idea for a bedtime story. "It wasn't there. And then it was." Eventually, if you told yourself the story enough times, as she would do over the coming weeks, its every thread seemed inevitable. These reflections, of course, would come later. Sitting in the salon chair, her hair matted in lather, all Abbie knew was that she'd found an alternative to a death of quiet desperation. The previous night, she'd counted barbiturates in preparation for a private end. Now a public departure rose before her, a dramatic gesture. That was the sort of hook you could hang your life on.

Abbie drew her head up. Soapy water trickled down her back.

"What the hell?" exclaimed Summer.

Abbie rummaged in her purse. She closed the girl's hand around three crisp twenty dollar bills.

"Fuck, honey," shouted Summer. "What's wrong?"

"I'm dying," Abbie answered, smiling.

She brushed past the stylist and hurried outside. It was a bright afternoon. The sidewalks were crowded. Some pedestrians glanced uncomfortably at Abbie, but most ignored her. She didn't care.

She walked home briskly, trailing water and suds up Ninety-First Street.

Bert's encounter with his ex-wife left him jittery. When he'd driven down to meet Abigail at St. Mary's, forty miles south of Chatham Valley, he'd hoped to knock off other errands. A college friend had recently acquired an étagère at a rummage sale. The man thought it might be valuable and had asked Bert to take a look. Also, Bert wanted to buy fresh oysters for Wes. And then there was the forgery case in which he was to be an expert witness, one of the perks of semi-retirement. For weeks, the lawyers had been on his back about dropping off the affidavits. Before visiting Abigail, Bert had planned to wipe clean his to-be-done list. Afterwards, of course, he'd been useless.

He found Wes out in the yard, digging a trench around his vegetable garden. This was the latest salvo in his war against woodchucks.

"You're home early," said Wes.

Bert dabbed his brow with his handkerchief. "What's that old Chinese curse? May you live in interesting times."

"That bad, eh?"

"Worse."

Bert recounted the morning's trauma. Wes continued to dig. He'd slung his t-shirt over a wooden fencepost, baring the lean muscle of his chest. At seventy, Wesley Rockford was still "the straightest gay man in the lower forty-eight." Sport fisherman. Hockey fan. One-time petrochemical engineer. (He claimed that in his native Alaska, some gay men were even straighter.) Wes had lost three fingers in a childhood hunting accident, leaving a right hand like a vintage baseball mitt. When he shoveled, he used only his left arm.

"It wasn't just the cancer," said Bert. "Or the suicide plan. It was all of it together. You had to see her there in that empty classroom—Those stacks of tiny chairs—Good God! She looked so...."

"Diminished?"

"Yeah," said Bert. "Diminished."

He sat down on the grass, using his jacket as a pillow. That portion of the lawn had been newly mowed. Later, Wes would rake up the clumps of fresh chaff.

"Abigail's mother was also a smoker," added Bert—to no particular purpose. "She also quit too late."

Wes kicked a clod of dirt off his shovel. He picked up a stone and lobbed it into the hedge. "Are you asking for advice?"

Bert shrugged. "Who knows? It hasn't sunk in yet."

"I imagine it hasn't. Are you sure she was serious?" Wes kneaded his lower lip between his fingers, a sure sign that he was concerned. "I never thought of your ex as so political. People have a way of talking when they're under stress—and they really don't mean anything by it."

"She was serious. As hard as that is to believe. Jesus Christ! This is something Buddhist monks do, not New York City school teachers." Bert wiped a tear from his eye. "Her sense of humor hasn't changed though—for better or for worse. She said that even a chef as bad as I am can rustle up Abigail Richmond flambé."

"I'm surprised she asked *you*," said Wes. "Doesn't she have anybody else?"

"Apparently not. Or maybe I wasn't her first choice," said Bert, although privately he was sure that he was the first person, the *only* person, that Abbie had asked for help, and this touched him deeply. "I guess she's at the end of her rope. Desperate times call for desperate measures—and all that."

Wes tossed his shovel into a mound of red earth. He settled onto the grass, resting the back of his neck against Bert's abdomen. They lay in silence. Wes's head rose and fell with Bert's breath. Bert knew they were sharing the same thought: How grateful they were that they were together—*that Bert had left Abigail*. Cleaning the attic the previous spring, Bert had discovered the letters he'd written to Wes in Alaska. Their urgency stunned him. Certainly, he'd never loved Abigail so intensely.

He ran a hand through Wes's thick gray hair. "I suppose I owe it to her," he said.

"You don't *owe* her anything," answered Wes. "But you should stop her."

"I don't know. It's not that simple."

"You're not actually thinking of helping her, are you?" demanded Wes. He sat up, his shoulders and neck rigid. "Are you out of your mind?"

Bert looked away. A bank of clouds rolled across the sky. Others hunkered at the horizon. Darker clouds, the color of steel wool. As a child, he'd had a knack for finding secrets in clouds—rabbits, dragons. In Pelican Bay, Florida. A long time ago.

"Don't think crazy," said Wes. "You can't go around setting people on fire. You could go to jail, Bert. You could ruin our lives."

Wes was right, Bert realized. Wes was nearly always right. It could ruin their lives. But hadn't he once done fare worse to Abbie?

"Let's go inside," he said. "Before it rains."

This was the first year of Bert's semi-retirement. Their friends had warned him against this arrangement. When you're ready, they said, go whole hog. Half-retired was like partially pregnant. Often, it meant premature idleness. Time would weigh heavily upon him. The reality—in his case—had been decidedly the opposite. He'd had too many offers, not enough hours in the day. He still undertook special projects for his former employer, the city's leading auction house. Insurance companies offered him lucrative consulting fees. A niche publisher wanted him to lend his expertise to a line of coffee table books. Bert didn't delude himself. He wasn't a household name. But by hook and by crook, he'd risen to the top of his field. Not shabby for the self-taught son of a pawnbroker.

"Maybe I feel guilty," he told Wes. "My life worked out. Hers didn't."

They were walking up Broadway toward Abigail's building. They were late. Parking had taken forever.

"Count no man happy until he dies," quoted Wes.

"Meaning?"

"It's Oedipus. Greek for 'Don't jinx us.'"

Bert grinned. He pressed Abigail's buzzer. Her building didn't have an elevator, so they walked up the six narrow flights of stairs. "Thank you for doing this," he said as they reached the topmost landing. He squeezed Wes's hand. "Thank you for *understanding*."

"Nobody said anything about *understanding*, Bertram" said Wes. "But I do love you—so if you're going to insist upon making a mess of things, I'm going to try my best to minimize the damage."

This was good enough, thought Bert. That first evening, Wes had argued and cajoled and pleaded. *What did Bert know about self-immolation? Wasn't he afraid of the consequences?* But Bert's partner was a practical man. When it became clear that Bert was seriously considering a part in this folly, Wes determined to keep him from getting caught. He'd insisted upon coming along to see Abigail—as much to keep an eye on Bert as to vet his ex-wife's plan.

Abigail greeted them at the door. She kissed Bert's cheek, shook Wes's hand. "Catch your breath," she said.

"I forgot how steep those stairs are," said Bert, coughing.

She laughed. "The cost of high ceilings."

The flat was just as Bert remembered. Tasteful, a tad stuffy. Walls and walls of Leonard's books. Several of the volumes were quite valuable. First editions of Freud, of Benjamin Rush, of Lister's essay on inflammation. A glass and mahogany bureau housed the sterling silver tea service that had once been Leonard's mother's. There was also a good share of kitsch: commemorative porcelain, bead bouquets, watercolor seascapes. The apartment's most interesting fixture—although of minimal commercial value—was a life-size plastic skeleton. It hung opposite the Laz-E-Boy recliner, where one expected to find a television set.

Abigail steered them into the dining room. She followed moments later with a tea pitcher and a plate of scones. "How long has it been, Wesley?" she asked. "You look spectacular."

"You do, too."

She poured the tea. "For a woman on the verge of death."

Bert and Wes exchanged looks. Abigail had always been a pale-skinned, curveless woman—but in a comely, country lass sort of way. Now she looked sallow and stiff like a tarnished candlestick.

"Take anything you want, by the way," she said. "I know there are some books that interested you, Bert. Help yourself."

"You know I can't do that," said Bert.

"Why not?" snapped Abigail.

Bert spooned sugar into his tea.

"I can't take them with me," Abigail persisted. "This isn't Ancient Egypt."

"You'll outlive us all yet," said Bert.

Abigail held her teacup only inches from her lips. "*No*," she said. "*I won't.*"

Bert added another spoonful of sugar to his tea. He took a small sip. It was too sweet. This visit no longer seemed a good idea. He'd hoped having Wes along would calm his nerves, but he wasn't as comfortable with helping Abigail as he'd claimed. He'd taken her to the high school prom, after all. And deep down, although he was grateful to Wes for tolerating this insanity, he realized that he was now mistreating Wes as he'd once mistreated Abigail. It was *their* life he might ruin. Not just his own. At the same time, a part of him sympathized with his ex-wife's plan. He *did* understand. Unlike Abigail, he had been political. He and Wes had rallied against the epidemic in the eighties. They'd marched for Matthew Sheppard. They'd done their part. And over the past month, he'd also become obsessed with the war news. He watched non-stop, religiously, hoping the conflict might end. If there were no war, there would be nothing to protest—no reason for Abigail to kill herself.

Other men might have searched for guidance in religion, or psychiatry, or the classics. These had never been part of Bert's life. Instead, he'd tracked down Abbie's son in Utah. First, Norman had hung up on him. When he phoned again, the son called him a shit-packing faggot. Bert saw no reason to mention this encounter to his ex-wife.

"Wes and I are thinking of traveling," said Bert.

Wes threw Bert a puzzled look. Abbie smiled. "That's terrific," she said. "You've certainly earned it."

"Does that mean...?"

She shook her head. "I can work around your schedule."

Bert reached his hand into his trouser pocket and fumbled with his keys. His strong suit was property, not people. As hard as he tried, he had a difficult time drawing a connection between Abigail and the bloodshed overseas. *Everybody* he knew opposed the war. It was something you opposed in the abstract—like inequality or injustice. But that didn't mean you had to sacrifice yourself. Abbie didn't even own a television. He doubted she could name both of their United States senators. Now that he was actually in her apartment, discussing her suicide as casually as a birthday party or retirement dinner, he want to shake her. He wanted to tell her that she was the second most important person in his world. To say how empty his life would be without her jibes, her quotations from Emerson and Whitman, her ravenous laugh.

Instead, he asked: "When?"

"Not just yet," said Abigail. "What is it they say after casting calls? Don't call us, we'll call you."

Abbie saw no need for immediate action. Occasionally, reading the names of fallen American servicemen in the morning newspaper, or contemplating the larger number of unreported foreign casualties, she was seized by a twinge of regret. Might she have saved these people? Had she cost some poor mother her son? But Abbie wasn't fool enough to believe that even her public burning could single-handedly alter national policy—that anything she'd have done would have mattered. Her goals were more modest, long-term. Also, she wasn't ready to die.

The first weeks of July, Abbie devoted to practical matters. She broke down her apartment as she'd done her classroom. Drawer by drawer, shelf by shelf. It amazed her how much junk she and Leonard had acquired over the years. A pair of pack rats. Now she gave it all away. The silver tea service and the medical books would go to Bert; she'd arranged it with the lawyer. Anything else of value—and who knew what had value these day!—was to be sold, the proceeds to St. Mary's. Abbie double-checked the perpetual upkeep on her parents' graves, gave the Dominican superintendent his Christmas tip on Bastille Day, bid silent farewell to her friends. Her death would be messy, explosive. She hoped to leave her affairs tied-up and tidy.

If anything scared her, it was the pain. At the age of eleven, she'd stuck a paperclip into an electric outlet. She still had a scar on her index finger. This, she feared, would be far worse. But as she learned more about Thich Quang Duc and his Vietnamese monks, about Jan Palach in Wenceslas Square, she discovered that self-immolation—like most specialized skills—had its own artistry. You couldn't grit your teeth and bear it, as you might an injection. The trick, it appeared, was to lose yourself in a fugue state. One authority compared it to long-distance running. Through much of August, Abbie explored the subject. She sat in the small island of lindens and plane trees, at the juncture of Broadway and West End Avenue, reading about Afghan brides and Tibetan monks and the Ananda Murga cult. If she'd had time—if life had taken another course—she might have pursued these studies academically. She could already envision the shape of her dissertation: chapters on Indian sati rituals and Turkish Kurds. But Abbie sensed she was growing weaker. She had trouble maintaining her balance, forming fists. Some days she didn't make it to the park or even out of her dressing gown. According to her oncologist, the cancer had spread to her brain.

Several times, Bert phoned. Dear Bert. "Just to check in." He wanted to discuss the war, but truthfully, the details of the fighting didn't interest her. She knew it was wrong. Deep down. *That* was what mattered. Why should she care for particular battles, the names of interchangeable generals? In college, she'd been rebuked for hazy thinking. Her history professor regarded her as pleasantly vapid. (Many years later, she'd run into the same professor at Tanglewood. *A third-grade teacher*, he'd said. *Important work.* She'd wanted to claw his eyes out.) If it were possible to miss anything once you were dead, she would miss Bert. His decency, his lavender handkerchiefs that looked like dinner napkins. And she'd miss children. Their tiny fingers, their solidarity. Being a second-rate classroom teacher, it was Abbie's curse to love young children so terribly.

The morning after Labor Day, Abbie rose early. She'd stayed up late the night before, enjoying the final pages of *The Forsyte Saga*. (She'd read somewhere that John Hinckley and Mark Chapman had carried *The Catcher in the Rye* with them. Maybe, she'd told Bert, she could inspire a new trend.) Outside, the air was damp. A nip of autumn already hung in the breeze. When Abbie arrived at St. Mary's, the children were already getting off the busses. One after another. In little yellow raincoats, carrying brown bag lunches. The light was on in Abbie's classroom. Through the bars, she could see the walls layered with construction paper. Orange. Green. Red. She walked to the pay telephone on the corner and called Bert.

It was time.

Bert picked Abigail up at the curbside. She wore tan slacks, a beige blouse, a matching kerchief. Her trademark canvas bag hung over one shoulder. She couldn't have weighed more than ninety pounds. On the phone, Abigail had warned him to expect the worst— but nothing could have braced him for the fragile steps, the bony cheeks, the sharp sinews exposed in her neck. Overnight, his ex-wife had suddenly become an old woman. A woman *beyond* a certain age. When she reached the car, he'd had to go around to help her close the door.

"Did you have any trouble?" she asked.

"Smooth sailing," he said. "So far."

He glanced in the rear-view mirror at the stack of press releases. These were to be distributed afterwards. The most critical resource, three canisters of gasoline, he'd concealed under a blanket in the trunk. Wes had provided him detailed instructions about covering his tracks—on the importance of handing the gas canisters with gloves and of shielding his license plates with burlap. Wes had purchased the envelopes for the press releases at a stationery shop in the next county, afraid that the FBI might trace the paper stock. He'd warned Wes to deposit them in multiple mail boxes. He loved Wes for taking on this deranged mission as his own. Yet even as they'd kissed on the doorstep that morning, Bert sensed that Wes was hoping he might reconsider. He nearly did.

"I'm glad it's September," said Abigail. "I've always looked forward to September."

Bert started the ignition, but drove slowly. "We could stop for some coffee," he said, as casually as possible. "Wait for the weather to clear."

"Wait until I lose my resolve. Is that it?" Abigail rolled down her window and surveyed the rain with her palm. "Barely anything. Just a drizzle."

They eased their way down Broadway. Block by block, light by light. Both of them aware that Bert had chosen the slowest route. On the drive from Chatham Valley, he'd had so much to tell Abigail. About him. About her. About them. Now his mind had gone blank. "Wes said to send his love," he said.

"Please thank him for me. I always liked Wesley."

Traffic slowed around Columbus Circle. Jaywalkers darted through the intersection. Cabs honked. Abigail had selected the front steps of Federal Hall for her departure. Across from the Stock Exchange. The site of Washington's Farewell Address. She'd considered City Hall Park, Ground Zero. (It was like choosing a venue for a wedding, only cheaper.) Ultimately, she'd sought a place without children. A vacationing family, she'd feared, might break her nerve.

"Maybe we should have had kids," said Bert.

Abigail smiled. Her eyes glowed. "Maybe."

Bert considered reaching for her hand, but didn't.

After that, they rode in silence. Bert watched Abigail while they drove; she gazed out the window, her hands folded in her lap. When they reached the Financial District, she said, "In *War and Peace*, Pierre almost assassinates Napoleon. But, in the end, he doesn't have it in him."

They were stopped at a traffic light. Bert turned to face her. He expected to see tears in her eyes, but they were dry. "If I don't have it in me…." she said.

She looked at him helplessly; her hands were shaking.

"Hush," he said. "It will go fine."

The night before, Wes had painted the gasoline canisters black. From a distance, they looked like stereo speakers or lighting equipment. They parked several blocks away—as far as Abigail could walk—and Bert carried the fuel along Wall Street. They advanced slowly, at Abigail's limited pace. The rain had tapered off, leaving a residue of soggy wrappers on the steps of Federal Hall. In one corner, a woman

Abigail's age fed pigeons. A band of twenty "permanent" anti-war protestors stood entrenched behind a nearby police cordon. Several wore tie-dyed t-shirts, shaggy beards. Others were better dressed, including one elderly man with a bowtie. They occasionally waved their political placards. Across the street, behind an identical cordon, an even smaller pro-war faction marched solemnly in a narrow circle. There was a young man in a naval dress uniform and a handful of homely, overweight girls draped in American flags. Bert genuinely felt badly for them—as he once had when he'd heard eighty year-old Barry Goldwater interviewed on public radio. Yet at least they believed in *something*, he thought, however misguided. Across the street, at the Stock Exchange, the lunchtime crowd was starting to file onto the streets.

"I'm not good at farewells," said Bert.

"Who is?" asked Abigail.

She handed him her canvas bag. How decisive it felt to take it from her. Soon enough he'd be meeting Wes at their bridge club, the alibi they'd chosen, and already the claiming of the body, and the funeral, and the plans for a spring unveiling–all carefully mapped out by Wes—now seemed inevitably. Nearly fait accompli.

Bert struggled to find the right words for the moment, but some moments were beyond mere words. Abigail nodded in the direction of the anti-war protestors. "The competition," she said.

"For you," answered Bert. "Absolutely no match."

Abigail smiled. She retrieved a tiny self-striker from a small rectangular box.

"The *perfect* match," she said, holding it up. "Now step back."

Abigail eased herself down to the steps and poured the gasoline over her head. First by tilting the canisters, then lifting them as they yielded weight. She might have been a small child enjoying a public bath. Bert couldn't bear to watch. He felt nauseous. He jostled his way along Wall Street toward Broadway.

Behind him, he heard shouting. He caught a glimpse of the flames reflected in the plate glass of a bakery window. It was done.

Now he was to dispatch the press releases and then meet Wes at the bridge club in Chatham Valley. Instead, he continued walking, running. He'd lost track of where he was heading or why.

He found himself crossing through Battery Park, approaching the water, the canyons of Lower Manhattan receding behind him. Songbirds flitted in the trees. Wes would have known their names. Across the harbor rose Ellis Island, The Statue of Liberty, New Jersey. Several small children were playing in the wet grass, illuminated by a thin white beam of sun. Bert stopped to watch them. It was a perfectly tranquil moment, the sort Abigail had treasured. This was why she'd sacrificed herself so willingly—not for an abstract peace, but for a moment just like this one, a moment of genuine grace for Bert and for humanity. You could close your eyes, and listen to the children's laughter, and imagine that nobody, anywhere, had ever died.

PORTER FOX

CARIBOU

I've seen fish fly. Up north where the softwood is so thick you can't walk the forest without an axe. I've seen a fourteen-inch brookie glide through the air, its paper tail feathering the breeze, sun glistening in its scales, sailing across the sky and headfirst smack into a snarl of beaks. Gripped in the osprey's talons, it goes like it was meant to go.

I've watched one of those birds dive at the water like a shadow on the highway then come alive with barbed talons, sinking them into the fish and can't let go. Once, Edison saw a twenty-inch brookie drag a bird right under.

Edison's hands are delicate as he packs—or they look delicate the way he wedges his rifle between the tent and duffel bags. There's a cooler lashed to the back of the cab, two plastic containers of camping supplies. Suzanne watches from the plywood steps leading to the kitchen.

There's no roof on the house, she says.

She's right. It's just plywood and tarps. The roof was supposed to be finished two months ago. But the closer Edison got to completing it, the slower he went. Now the first cold has settled. The snow won't be far behind.

You see the special last night? I ask.

On the boys? Edison says.

Caribou.

He looks at Suzanne, me. We'll be fine, he says.

Just wondered if you saw it.

What'd it say?

They're moving south. It hit ten below on the Gaspé last night.

Sounds about right.

They say it's the earliest migration yet. Scared off half the hunters in the lottery.

I best get moving then.

They say to keep to the roads.

I doubt there are many caribou on the roads.

You know how it gets up there.

A snowflake twirls into the garage and lands on the concrete floor. Edison watches it fall, glances at Suzanne, steps into the cab.

They find those boys? he asks.

Not yet, I say.

Then they won't.

You don't know that.

*

I've seen incredible things in the North Woods. Like Luke Jenson bend a tire iron over his knee for no reason. I once saw Frank Pelletier eat a light bulb to impress a girl. I've watched the sawyers jump off the roof of the Northland Saloon in the middle of winter, land on their backs in the parking lot, stand up, brush themselves off and walk away. Or Edison. He walks a three-day trap line in the middle of February with nothing but a bag of jerky, an axe, his snowshoes and a blanket.

It's this country that makes them—the mountains circling Three Forks like emerald waves, pine forests reaching to the Atlantic, spruce and fir hemming our yards like they're waiting to reclaim them.

And the cold. The lakes freeze in November and thaw in May. The air burns your lungs in the middle of January. At night, the streetlights shine straight up instead of down. The northern lights glow over the mountains early in the morning. One night when it hit forty below I saw a doe freeze solid in my yard. I walked up to her the next day and pushed her over. She just stared at me, legs sticking straight out to the side.

We were all born here. We'll probably be buried here. We're too far from anything to think about leaving. Seven miles from Canada, three hundred to the Atlantic. But that doesn't mean we belong here. I'm not sure anyone belongs where the ground is frozen ten months of the year.

An orange streetlamp buzzes outside my apartment. I have a suitcase of beer and a half-packed duffel on the living room floor. I wonder what's stopping me. Familiarity, fear. Sometimes when a nor'easter blows through the treetops, it sounds like the whiskbroom of God trying to sweep us from the forest.

Family Feud is on. There's no money to be won. Just a couple hundred bucks on the board and a cute brunette. The news breaks in to say something about the boys. They disappeared two weeks ago hunting on the Gaspé. The reporter says they're twenty and twenty-three years old. They won the license lottery on their first try. It took Edison eight years.

It's never been this cold this early. The newscaster says the boys got caught on the southeast coast of the Gaspé; four feet of snow fell on the road behind them. They didn't have radios, phones, food. It'll be a miracle if they find them. And the weather's not getting any better. There's mares' tails up there, a cold front coming in from the north.

Edison said he'd clear my debt if I finish the roof for him. That's fair. He owns half my truck and I'm going to need it. I've been looking for jobs in Florida. Key Largo. Something on the water. They say there's two feet of beach for every person down there.

*

Suzanne sets the table for two the night Edison leaves. She lays plastic utensils on squares of paper towel folded in half. The roof tarps ripple as the front moves through. Webs of frost spread across the windows. I see her reflection—auburn hair, hazel eyes, a veiled sex Edison's described but you'd be a fool to miss. She says I'm family, that she's told me most everything about her. But Edison's told me more. Half-dead in a frozen lake when she was four. A mother who drank like a sawyer. A talent for meeting the wrong man at the right time.

Edison tells me everything. I've known him since I could walk. I've never seen him back down from anything. I've never seen him give something up for free either. He keeps his tabs. To him, love is being on hand when he needs you.

I've seen Suzanne at the Northland with Sam Fuller. I don't know what that means, but I know Edison doesn't know anything about it. Or maybe he does. People can live two lives up here and the town will only talk about one. Like Mr. Peterson who steals from the general store. Or Ms. Doyle whose cats keep disappearing. I've got a different life with Suzanne. I know it and I think she does too. Sometimes I wonder if it's all right, or if it's just me making something out of nothing. It doesn't matter. It's all just talk.

*

Suzanne's asleep when I start tacking down the plywood sheathing the next morning. I rig a block and tackle to lift the sheets to the roof. The trusses and rafters are secure. All I have to do is nail down the plywood, roll out the ice-and-water shield, run the flashing, then shingle. It shouldn't take more than a week, but it's supposed to drop below zero on Friday so I might not have a week. On the way to Edison's that morning I noticed skim ice creeping across the lake.

The plywood is frozen and heavy. I pull on the rig, loop the rope once around my wrist and yank each piece to the roofline. Once I get a sheet up, I tie off the rope, slide the plywood into place and tack it down.

You get right to it, Suzanne says an hour into the job. She's standing in the living room wearing sweatpants and a State Fair T-shirt.

I've never seen the lake freeze so fast, I say.

Or a house.

She disappears into the kitchen. I tack down the last piece in the row and by the time I get a new sheet rigged up, Suzanne returns with a mug of coffee.

Don't say I didn't warn you, she says.

That night Suzanne cooks trout. She puts two lit candles on the table. I can smell the fish broiling as I finish tacking the first half of the roof under a tar-black sky.

Edison ought to put a statue of you in the yard, she says when we sit down.

If he wanted to keep people out.

You're saving his marriage.

Least I could do.

Two brook trout sit on a platter between us. They're browned with the head still on. Suzanne smiles, raises her glass.

To my husband's hunting vacation, she says.

I nod and she sips her wine.

When's he coming back? I ask.

When he gets a bull, or divorce papers.

He'll get one.

Which?

A bull.

Suzanne slides one of the fish onto my plate.

What's this I hear about moving south? she asks.

Spring, I say. Florida.

Edison's going to miss you.

I'm not going to miss this.

Suzanne strips the meat off her fish and lifts a forkful to her mouth. A country song plays on the radio. She taps her fork to the rhythm.

I think it's time *I* got a vacation, she says.

Where?

Zanzibar.

What the hell's that?

White beaches and blue lagoons.

She slides her hands across the table and I see emerald water and alabaster sand spread across the checkered tablecloth.

Fruit trees, she says.

Margaritas?

Bathtub water.

A moth flutters into a candle and drops onto the table.

I've heard lagoons down south can be a thousand feet deep, I say.

After dinner we watch the late news. The boys are still lost. The temperature is dropping and the Quebec government has issued a warning. The local consensus is that there's no way the boys could still be alive. The reporter interviews a group of hunters who're headed home. One of them lost a toe to frostbite. Another group got lost yesterday but found their way out. The scene cuts to the boys' parents at the search-and-rescue center. It's in a construction trailer. There are radios and bright orange jackets along the wall and two coffeemakers in the corner.

The boys' parents look tired, furrowed brows, graying hair. One of the mothers is crying. The reporter asks her what viewers can do to help.

Pray, she says.

I wash the dishes while Suzanne watches T.V. The moon is rising. It makes the snow look blue. I can see the corner of the garage through the window, the rows of split cordwood behind it. Each stack stands five feet high. They're straight and neat with half logs on the ends.

A coyote runs across the lawn. It pauses near the corner of the garage, gazes into the living room. It's mangy and has beady eyes. I turn to tell Suzanne and it runs into the woods.

By the end of the week, I have all the plywood up and the soffits hung. It's twenty below at night, but Suzanne keeps the stove full and the house is warm enough. She cooks fish or steak for dinner every night and I start sleeping in the La-Z-Boy so I don't have to drive home. In the morning, I wear a ski hat and gloves to roll the ice-and-water shield. By Sunday I've got the roof covered and Monday afternoon I run the flashing. The long strips of metal flicker in the sun. The sky is deep blue and the mares' tails have blown out. The lake is completely covered in ice now. Someone's already dragged an ice-fishing shack to the landing.

*

Suzanne climbs the ladder Tuesday afternoon to see how I'm doing. She's carrying two Bloody Marys.

You know I don't drink on the job, I say.

You won't have a job if you don't follow orders.

Yes ma'am.

I help her onto the roof and take one of the plastic glasses.

It's nice up here, she says.

I could use another set of hands.

I'm not touching this roof.

He would've done it if he had time.

Time was never the issue.

He's not good at finishing things.

Don't tell me.

You hear anything from him?

What do you think?

You knew what you were getting into the first night you met him.

You could've reminded me.

I pick at a staple sticking out of the roof and sip my drink. Suzanne finishes hers. The air smells like sawdust and tar. The sun is an orange globe just over the trees.

What do you think about fate? she asks.

What do you mean?

Do you believe in it?

I don't know.

I could have just as easily walked up to you that night.

You didn't, I say.

This could've been your house.

It's not.

Could've been.

Anything could've been.

That's all I'm saying.

We don't talk through dinner. I turn on the T.V. and watch the second half of a special on Egypt. Suzanne brings the bottle of vodka to the living room and tops off her drink. I hand her mine and she pours a shot. Then she kicks off her shoes and lies on the couch. I recline in the La-Z-Boy and drift off after a few minutes. I dream about the lake, caribou, the sun setting over the ocean. When I wake, Suzanne's standing over me.

Is it true? she asks.

What?

About the lagoons.

Who?

They can be a thousand feet deep?

How would I know?

She tucks her hair behind her ear and walks to the kitchen. She comes back with a glass of water and leaves it next to the chair. Then she leans to kiss me on the cheek, but my head turns and she kisses my eye. She steps back and smiles. Then she walks upstairs. I pull an afghan over me and listen to a maple branch tap against the kitchen window. Blue moonlight pushes through the trees. I wonder if Edison got a bull yet then I fall asleep.

*

It doesn't take much to get lost up here. Take thirty steps into the woods and turn yourself around a dozen times. The only landmarks are the fire tower on McEwen Hill and the highway—if you can see them. When you're deep in the softwood, about all you can make out are your feet below you and your axe in your hand.

I got lost once. It was in the draw behind Crocker Lake. I'd been looking after Edison's trap line while he was away and got turned around. I thought I'd walked up one side of a saddle and down the other, when I'd actually walked back down the same side. All the trees looked the same. The brook was running in the right direction. Two days later I walked across the Union Pacific tracks twenty miles east of town.

I start shingling Tuesday afternoon and am done by Friday. I lay a clean drip edge with a twelve-inch overlap. It's overkill, but I don't want to leave yet. Suzanne has been going out in the morning, returning after I'm gone. I'm not sure if there's something awkward between us or if she's just worried about Edison. Friday night I start sleeping at home to give her space. When I finish the last row Sunday, I pack up my tools and drive home.

The Red Sox are playing the Orioles in the division series that night. The Sox have a young kid, Wilanski, who's supposed to be the next Yaz. He's nineteen and grew up in Rhode Island. He's like a prince in New England. He strikes out in the first and third innings then hits a monstrous three-run homer in the fourth. The crowd stands, the ball clears the upper deck. The boy runs the bases, his big arms swinging as he strides. He tips his helmet at home plate.

After the game, the news comes on. The anchor says the boys have been found. They were in the cab of their truck, huddled together. They'd frozen to death, he said. At the end of the report he adds another party to the missing list. A picture of Edison's face flashes on the screen.

I call Suzanne and get no answer. Then I turn off the T.V. and sit on the couch. The streetlamp buzzes outside. There isn't any wind. Just the moon and the blue light. I look out the window and see someone has dragged three fishing shacks to the middle of the lake.

*

The next day I go to Edison's to clean up the work site. Suzanne hasn't called and she isn't at the house when I arrive. I pile the extra plywood behind the garage, throw the flashing, tarpaper and shingles in the back of my truck. As I'm walking out the front door, she pulls into the driveway. She smiles and rolls down her window.

Hello stranger, she says.

You all right?

I've been better.

She turns off the car, looks at her lap, taps her fingers on the wheel.

Any word? I ask.

I've been at the warden's all morning.

Nothing?

It's been thirty-five below since Thursday.

Is it going to break?

There's another storm rolling in tonight.

That man never did anything half-ass.

Suzanne doesn't answer. She opens her door, steps out and reaches for a grocery bag in the passenger's seat.

Looks like you're cooking for two, I say.

See you 'round, she says and walks inside.

*

The last game of the series is on tonight. Wilanski triples and comes home on a sacrifice fly. The Sox have been on the road for two weeks and he looks tired. One of the announcers says he used to be a major league pitcher. Same thing night after night, he says. It wears you down.

I can't concentrate after the third inning and turn off the T.V. The streetlamp outside my window buzzes. I look for a beer in the fridge, stare at the lake. There's twelve ice sheds now, a little path between them. Last year someone put a stop sign on one end of the path. On New Year's day, Luke Jensen dressed up in a Santa Claus suit and directed traffic.

I pack the rest of my things into the duffel. There's not much—

some underwear, T-shirts, a few pairs of jeans. I put my shoes and some knickknacks from the bedroom in a trash bag and pile it all in the cab of the truck. Then I drive to the Northland to say goodbye.

Five sawyers lean against the vertical pine panels lining the far wall. Suzanne and Sam Fuller are huddled together at the end of the pool table. They're playing as a team. The lights aren't very bright so the bartender hangs a green Coleman lantern over the table. It hisses and casts a sharp, white light.

Sam lines up a shot and sinks it. Suzanne grabs him and kisses him on the cheek. Sam blushes then knocks another solid into the corner pocket. When Suzanne sees me she runs over and wraps her arms around my waist.

What are you doing? I ask.

I made three!

I look around the bar again and Sam turns to talk to the sawyers.

Let's go, I say.

Lemme finish my game.

I pay for Suzanne's drinks and walk her to my truck. I drive slow mostly because of the black ice on the road, but also because I'm not sure what's happening.

They found him, Suzanne says.

What?

They found him. This afternoon. I got a call.

Where?

Right where they stopped. They're fine.

All of them?

The warden called me.

Suzanne rests her head in my lap. I try to focus on the road and follow a loop past the dump and back to town. I make the turn the next time around and when I stop, Suzanne is motionless. I whisper to her, then carry her inside and up to her bedroom. I take off her shoes and pull the covers over her. Then I walk downstairs and load the stove.

The ladder I used is still leaning in the corner. I take it outside and climb onto the roof. The shingles sparkle in the moonlight. They're straight and spaced well. The drip edge is a little long, but Edison should be happy.

I climb down and walk inside to the La-Z-Boy. Then I go upstairs. Suzanne's asleep and snoring quietly. Edison's shoes sit beside his dresser. The dim red numbers on his digital clock flip to two thirty-three. I strip down and slide in beside her. The wind moves through the trees. The sound is like paper shuffling. It's so soft, you wouldn't hear it unless you were listening for it.

*

It's cold when I wake. The fire's gone out. Six inches of snow has fallen. It's not dawn yet. I get out of bed and Suzanne rolls onto her side. Downstairs I put on Edison's overalls and boots and jacket. Then I stomp a path to the woodpile.

I take a couple half logs off the end and balance one on a rotting stump. Edison's axe feels light in my hands and I come awake as the oiled handle slips through my fingers. The sound of the blade hitting the wood echoes through the forest.

After I load the fire, I change into my own clothes and get into the truck. The duffel and garbage bag are on the floor. I drive past the Northland toward the lake and stop at the landing. An ice fishermen shuffles between two shacks. The wind lifts a swirl of snow around one of them.

I drive onto the lake and the snow squeaks under the tires. I ease down on the gas and pass the shacks. Snow billows from the wheel wells and in a minute I'm going forty. There are three-foot drifts every hundred yards and when I hit one it explodes over the hood and up onto the windshield.

I roll down my window and let the snow and cold in. It's freezing but the sun is warm. I close my eyes. This is how it used to be around here. Nothing to hit. Just the trees and water and the caribou before the hunters pushed them north. The old timers say the big herds gathered in the valley in the fall. The cows stayed as long as they could, feeding on the tall grass and lichen around the lake. When it got too cold, they started south with the calves. Then the bulls would follow, two weeks behind, all of them in a long line just a few days before the first snow.

WANDERING BOY

JAMES GISH, JR.

It was six-thirty when my father finished lubing Dreck Benson's old Buick and took it off the rack . I pumped four dollars worth of high test for Butch Tobe and gave him a dollar in change. He mumbled but didn't look at me. The wind from off the river tumbled trash and candy wrappers down the street.

Half a block down, Mrs. Henson turned on the IGA sign. In the bleak grayness of the early January evening, it was a yellow smudge . Dreck Benson paid and left. I turned off the kerosene heater over by the RC machine. My father turned off the gas pumps with a switch inside the door.

"Sleet in the air, Dooley?"

"Yes sir. I can smell it."

We did not have to turn off the radio. My father told the mechanics, Ron and Pete, that it had a burned out tube. They just nodded. They knew better.

The old, green International pickup growled and spit, then started. We went out along Turner and then up Elm. Past the Texaco station where Denver Reese waved and Billy Cheatum lit a cigarette and pretended not to see us.

All the time I was thinking of those other days when Benny Jo rode with us. Talking about baseball or calling out to Francine Drell or Patty Majors, maybe wondering when he would get those straight pipes he wanted for that green over white Pontiac my father let him have. And even though it was five years ago, when I was eleven, if I closed my eyes, I could still see him there. His shock of unruly dark hair and that intense way of squinting ahead like he knew something wonderful and precious which he was not quite ready to tell everyone just yet.

At the Calvary Baptist, my father parked behind Reverend Cates' station wagon and went to tell him that we would be missing the regular Wednesday night prayer meeting for the first time in twelve years if you don't count the spring flood eight years ago.

Thirty or forty of us scattered out there on those scarred, oak benches, facing the front and that big Baptist Creed. Quoting scripture and giving thanks. Strangers in a strange land, the Book says. Huddled together , beset by cares and trials unbidden, wrestling with our faith like Jacob with the angel.

But not us tonight, things being how they were.

Out on Miller's Hill, we stood apart, him on one side of the grave and me on the other. Talking to ourselves, talking to her.

"I am sorry ,Lucille," my father said quietly. "The man with the salesman's voice said they would do it at midnight down there at Eddyville."

He stood there, shaking his head, his eyes closed.

"I got a 'B' on an Algebra quiz, Mama," I told her. "Annie called last night. She said the baby was colicky. It 's going to sleet tonight. Maybe they will call off school."

I twisted my red handkerchief in my hands. Four ducks lifted off a pond and flew south. I walked over and sat in the truck, watching the low dark clouds, racing each other across the lower sky like heavy smoke.

It was a hard thing to watch my father like this. He'd always had enough courage and certainty that it spilled over and he could give it away. Now he was lost on this high, cold plain of tragedy and doubt which he could not turn from or pray his way around.

I have seen him sitting in the counsel of fools, and when they had spoken whatever outlandish things their fevered brains could spawn, my father would nod as though he understood. Then, like some fantastical spider of magical design, he would take their ideas and weave them into a hundred separate threads of logic and something near truth. In the end, he would send them on their way, satisfied that they had spoken their piece and been heard clean and true.

But that was all gone now. This thing with Benny Jo had eaten at his soul like quick poison.

The wind whistled in the cracks of the windows. My father got in, rubbing his hands.

"Her grave is still sinking."

"It's that red clay," I said.

We drove home without talking. I watched out the window to the wasted corn fields full of rotting yellow stalks. I thought of us, my father, Benny Jo and me, walking there in the crisp colors of September. Of Benny Jo flushing out a quail and yelling, "Get that lead bird, Dooley."

At home, I put coal in the stove and went out to shovel some corn to the pigs. They squealed and fought in the mud, crowding out the runts. I pumped the trough full of water, knowing it would have a skin of ice by dusk. Back inside, I read the sports page and read my father a story about Stan Musial while he fried some bologna and eggs. We heard a car laboring up the lane, and I saw the sheriff's car pull to stop by that puny maple sapling I had pulled up two year's ago in Vanover's woods.

Lehman Buford, a Penacostal deacon and the county sheriff, stood over just inside the back door. His hands worked the brim of his hat.

"They are sending him home tomorrow night on the L&N, Darnell."

My father nodded.

"Me and Dooley will be there waiting in the pickup. I done got the burial permit through Maynard's office. They going to let us bury him back in that old over growed family plot back near that willow pond. Thanks for helping me walk through that red tape."

"You'd done it for me," Lehman told him with half a sigh.

"Sure you don't want some coffee. Dooley made a fresh pot not more than half an hour ago."

"Guess not. It gives me nerves. I'd be up watching them sing the National Anthem on Channel 7."

Then he was out the door. A minute later, I heard his wheels spinning in that deep rut out by the mailbox, the one we keep meaning to dump a load of gravel in but just never get around to it.

After we ate, my father said that he was going out to check on the stock. I told him okay, that I would do the dishes, even though I knew he was just going to go out in the barn and climb up there in the loft. He would sit on a hay bale and watch across the fields toward the river. Thinking of his oldest son some where in a dim, gray cubicle, watching the clock until the warden and priest came for him. And knowing my father, I knew that he was wondering where he had gone wrong. Wondering what he could have said to intervene, thinking of all those times he was busy until midnight putting on new brakes shoes or working two jobs, the farm and the lumber yard.

I did my homework, Spanish and Algebra. the words and figures swarmed and blurred. After a while, I heard the mantel clock ticking loudly and the soft squeak of that rocking chair my Uncle Harley had made from green wood, where my father found himself a steady rhythm, pacing himself for the long evening. He would be looking at the picture of my mother, who had wasted away with cervical cancer, out of her head with pain and medication, telling my sister to get the cake out of the oven and telling Benny Jo not to kill that black snake. Singing in those last days over and over, that same plaintive Appalachian chant "…where is my wandering boy tonight? The boy of my tenderest care?"

We went to bed early. At ten forty, the phone rang. I scrambled down the stairs to answer it, my feet cold on the wooden floor. It was my sister Annie from up near Louisville, her voice soft and slurred. She was crying and talking, all of it mixed together.

"Don't carry on so, Pig," I called her by my father's nickname for her.

"The man on the phone said we could have gone down to be there for him."

"You know he wouldn't want that. Daddy wouldn't go anyway. Said it was morbid to go watch people kill your own blood."

She was off the phone a second, and I heard ice cubes tinkle in a glass.

"It's like I'm in a dream , Dooley. It's like this can't be happening to me."

I held my tongue, resisting the impulse to tell her that it was not happening to her, that it was happening to Benny Jo, that it was happening to all of us. But we were both half muddled and dream-gaited. It didn't matter. So I sat on the stairs and picked at a raveling on my pajamas.

"Maybe if he'd got that job on the barge or got that scholarship to Murray State and hadn't busted his knee on that hay wagon. If damned Nettie Scales had not moved into town and wound him around her finger."

I heard myself and thought it sounded like a petulant child, mad at the fates and whining over bad fortune as though that was something meant only for others.

"Nettie Scales was shot four times, Dooley. Billy Deems was shot twice in the heart," my sister told me these things I knew already .

"Benny Jo wouldn't hurt a fly," I told her in weak counterpoint.

What I did not say while we held those silent phones across the miles was what I had thought to say to my father but then bitten back. That the Benny Jo who came back from Louisville for two Christmases was not the same Benny Jo who left us. It was as if the old Benny Jo had been eaten up whole and digested by this new creature who drank whiskey out of the trunk of his car late at night after my father went to bed. The kind of person who lived in a rat trap apartment in a bad part of the city and lay at night, grinding his teeth while his nightmares rode in full stride over the remnants of his dreams which were as thin and blue as vapor.

I listened to the sleet ticking off the roof, glazing the trees and roofs and roads.

Annie cried some more and hung up. I went back up to my room and lay there, trying to sleep. But it was near midnight now, and I was seeing the people come to his cell and lead him down that corridor. I got out of bed and turned on the lights. I had two old pictures of Benny Jo tucked in a yellow envelope in my night stand. I sat on the edge of the bed and looked at them. In one, he was maybe eight years old, wearing a straw hat and clenching his teeth around my grandfather's corn cob pipe. In another, he was sitting on Uncle Eldon's Harley, looking sideways at the camera and smiling that smile you would expect from a golden boy, who had always expected that earth's bounty was descending to crown him alone for all his considerable worth.

When I closed my eyes, I could see him, coming out of the river at his baptism.

His face all holy and full of light as Brother Cates said the scriptures and raised him up from the waters of the Ohio there near Scuffletown. On the shore, we sang a ragged harmony "Shall We Gather at the River." When Benny Jo broke the water, he came up radiant , like he was a saint who had been in a cave a long time and had himself a vision of wild angels.

*

When my alarm went off at six, I crawled out of bed in a daze. I sat there on the side of the bed, watching the snow fly outside the window. What sleep I had gotten was spotty, slippery sleep, full of turbulence and sudden wakings. I did not have to be told that my father had spent the night in a lonely vigil, either in his room , flat on his back.

Or in the living room, rocking there in the darkness, swarmed upon by midnight doubts which flitter flutter like gnats which do not rest and will not go away.

I went into the dark bathroom and splashed my face with cold water, then down to start the coffee. My father was already out in the barn, milking the tan cow named Susie. The electricity had gone off during the night because the ice and sleet had snapped a power line or some hurry-scurry worker from the Alcoa plant locked his brakes on a tight curve and clipped off a power pole.

I heard the creaking of the back door and watched him coming in with the milking pail, a towel draped over it .

"No school today," he told me as he poured the milk into the separator and put on the tin lid to keep out the occasional lazy winter fly which spawned in the walls and crawled out of that crack above the cook stove.

As we sat there at the table, stirring our coffee, thinking our separate thoughts which were only variations of the same thing, my father broke the silence.

"That your sister who called last night?"

"Yes, sir. It was her?"

"Was she making sense?"

It was a question fraught with his own knowledge of her nervous problems and her cure for them.

"As much as ever," I told him dismissively.

He stood up and got out a roll of sausage..

"She's just high strung. Maybe it would help if she married somebody who didn't teach her that bourbon whiskey is a good way to set the stars straight."

I nodded to him and scrambled some eggs in a bowl while he fried the sausage.

My mother would have fixed biscuits, but neither of us ever got past bad toast. We ate in silence and washed the dishes, putting them away carefully. It surprised our occasional visitor that two males living alone kept such a clean house. I think we just picked up what Mama had left us, some part of her kept alive in our rituals . It was a spare household, not a hint of real color except for the knick knacks she left us, some Depression glass and a See Rock City cream pitcher.

"You mind missing school and basketball practice?" my father asked as he wiped off the table.

"No. We got two teachers out on leave, and the coach is so busy trying to save his marriage, we mostly coach ourselves."

We fumbled around a few more minutes, both of us in and out of the kitchen. Finally, he asked if I wanted to pray with him, and we got down on our knees. I listened to his words, tracing them over in my head like you can do if you grow up in a house and hear the same person pray over and over. Like a litany of sorrows and worries- the widows and orphans, the soldiers on foreign soil, those who have dwelt in our mercy and our love. Benny Jo just there around the corner of the words not said.

We got up from our knees, and the lights buzzed back on.

"I think I will go up in my room , son. My head hurts some."

"Yessir. I'm going out to that squirrel tree near the new ground."

I began to put on my coveralls and heavy boots. I got my .22 from the gun rack. I could hear my father's steps upon the stairs, heavy and slow. I walked out the back door and across the horse lot and took a tractor trail along the ridge toward the river, a hard ball of ice in my stomach.

I went down to where Simpson's Branch emptied into the Green River and sat on a rotting log and watched some barges go by, kicking up muddy waves which lapped against the bank. On a sycamore tree a few yards away, I could still make out where Benny Jo had carved a heart with the name of a girl whom he had loved and then forgot or she had forgotten him. Down the bank two hundred yards, near the ferry slip, Benny Jo jumped into the water and pulled me out on my eighth birthday where I had got caught in a strong current. He carried me to the bank, cursing and crying because he was the big brother who was in charge, and he was suppose to keep me out of harm's way. He lay me in some muddy sand near a burned out campfire and pushed on my belly until I coughed up dark muddy water and then began to breathe. Then he went over and threw up in the horseweeds.

*

At seven-thirty that night, my father called up the stairs to say that Mr. Heppler at the train station had phoned. My father started the pickup, and we drove into town, sliding and creeping on the icy roads, both of us catching our breath and praying the truck out of those long slides where your stomach starts to turn. We parked the truck in that broken blacktop and went into the cavernous interior of the railroad station where the paint flaked off the walls and the exit signs had faded nearly out completely. The station had been built in the '40's to handle the troop trains to Fort Breckenridge and Fort Campbell.

Three old men from down county were there, sitting around a pot bellied stove, spitting tobacco juice into the coal bucket and throwing us furtive looks.

We went out on the platform with the sheriff, and he got Posey, the black porter, to get us a big loading dolly. In a few minutes, we could see the piercing beam from the front of the engine, and then it had chuffed to a stop. Three passengers disembarked, and then Posey led us to a baggage car where we wrestled the coffin down onto the dolly and then rolled it to the truck. As we slid the cheap, wooden coffin into the rusted bed, my father said, "Watch them sharp corners. You'll lose a finger."

I started to cry , but nobody mentioned it. My father shook hands with the sheriff, and he gave Posey two dollars.

Posey held up his hand and shook his head.

"I won't take money, Mr. Darnell. That boy was a ring tail wonder. I'd drag that box all the way to your house just for the strength of your son's good, long laugh."

"Okay, Posey," my dad said. "Thank you."

My father shook hands with the sheriff.

"Thanks, Lehman. I appreciate your help. I know this falls outside of your official duties."

Lehman Buford clapped him on the shoulder.

"Darnell, you're a Baptist, and I am a Pentecostal, and we have both seen the mouth of temptation. What I done was in recognition that could have easily been one of my own."

"No matter what you heard, he was a good boy," my father said, his voice suddenly gone weak and old.

The sheriff nodded and turned to go, but he turned back once more.

"You done all you could do, Darnell. Five years from now, I will remember him hitting eight foul shots in a row in the district finals and beating Beaver Dam at the gun with that half court shot. I will remember him in the seventh grade when he got beat up by that Thurston bully for standing up for my daughter."

We drove home with the radio on.

"Your true lovin' Daddy is movin' on," Hank Snow sang.

We parked the truck under the skeletal limbs of the slippery elm next to the smoke house. We had a certificate to bury him in the old family plot down by the pond where the snake doctors danced over the cattails in full summer. The church had a secret vote and asked that we not to bury Benny next to mama. Daddy said that it was all right. He'd figured it would happen, given what was on the radio and in the newspapers.

I went up to my room with a bologna sandwich and a glass of milk. I finished it and lay there on my bed with my clothes on, feeling a heavy fatigue welling up in my bones. I dozed and I dreamed of Benny Jo and Annie. In that sepia dream, I saw them bow to each other and then begin to dance. It was in our sideyard , over next to the apple trees. Snow began to fall about them, and they danced on, floating there among the snow flakes, like mythical creatures of great joy.

When I woke up, it was because I heard the car motor outside and then the door slam. I knew that it was Annie. Standing at the window, I saw my father come off the porch and go to take her in his arms, almost as though he had been sitting in the living room , waiting for those car lights to brighten the front window. Annie lurched a little, but Daddy caught her. I could hear her voice just a half note off hysteria. My father led her out to the pickup where he left her, leaning against the side, her head over on the cold wood of the coffin.

I should have gone to bed and given her privacy for mourning, but I did not. I stood there at the window, thinking of Benny Jo and Annie, growing up here in these upper rooms, their lives so pregnant with promise.

Then that other thought came, something so hard edged and true that it nearly took my breath away. What was my father thinking now? Was he watching me every day, not even fooled by what I said or pretended to be, always wondering when this last child would take some twisty turn and reveal that thing in himself which had gone sad and bitter at the core. Another monument to my father's endless prayers and all those good intentions.

That was when I heard the noise in his room. A keening moan like some beast yoked to a burden which he had dragged like a rock too long but had gone on pulling it until this terrible moment, when he had seen the breadth and depth of his own hopelessness and despair.

I leaned my head against the window, willing the noise to cease. That was when I saw Annie as she began to struggle with the awkward weight of the coffin, pushing, shoving and hauling it until , by some unthinkable feat of strength, she leveraged it from the bed of the pickup. As I watched, half fearful and half fascinated, she dragged Benny Jo's coffin inch by inch until it was beside the apple tree where I had dreamed the dance.

She disappeared from view for a few seconds, and when she reappeared, she was wearing what looked to be my brother's old basketball letter jacket and the crown she had worn as the home coming queen.

She commenced like a crippled bird, leaping and jigging as her heels flung up tufts of dead grass and dirt, stumbling and falling, but always back up again. She shook her fists skyward, as though daring God to show his face and offer the least hint of his best defense.

GREGORY LOSELLE

BURIED DINNER

It starts about a foot below the surface. First maybe a movie ticket—the thick old cardboard kind, the ones that last forever under ground like the newspapers you can dig up now and then in trash dumps—the headlines, the pictures still visible, the dates and captions, the stories you can still read—even the weather from whenever they were printed. It's something in the paper, maybe—or the soil—they hardly even turn brown under there, even if they're wet and the print shows through to the other side of the paper, and if they're folded, then they might as well be fresh yesterday.

Another six inches and it's a box lid from a Whitman's sampler or maybe an old 45 like the kind you only bring out on a first date—or maybe amusement park trash like those little colored aluminum disks with letters you can stamp on. These you definitely can read and they all say stuff like *JOHN AND CANDI—TRUE LOVE FOREVER*' like the sort of things kids carve on picnic tables and counters in school lunchrooms. The sort of stuff we all tell each other when we're in love—the same words almost every time, the same way of saying them. Nobody gets too original with these things.

After another foot or so a plastic fork or spoon turns up with a sandwich wrapper or a Styrofoam box like the kinds of stuff you can buy at a deli comes in. Maybe a few soda cans or a wine bottle, depending on whether this was at lunch or after work, and the little clear plastic cups that double for wine glasses at outdoor parties. Maybe even the cellophane from a bunch of flowers bought quick on the sidewalk from one of those drive-up stands: still rolled up, a few sprigs of baby's breath still inside. And then you know that's the second or third date—the picnic in the park, all the trash left behind so it's nice and clean: no dishes to bring home, no evidence, no chance the husband doing yard work will find out if he accidentally spills the garbage that day I first started digging down the side of the outside wall, following the crack in the cement all the way down to the foundation.

My mother comes out onto the porch and stares at the sky. The screen door slams behind her. I keep digging as she stands there, one hand on her hip and the other holding up a greasy spatula, like a sword. "It smells like rain," she says. The wind stirs the hem of her dress.

"Yeah."

She waves the spatula back at the house. "Lunch'll be done in a minute. Get cleaned up and I'll have it all ready." She turns and goes back inside. Because I'm right outside the basement wall I can hear her footsteps through the living room and into the kitchen. I toss another shovelful of dirt up and hoist myself up to the edge of the hole.

Sitting on the grass, I can see the crack better; it starts out as a hairline at the edge of the dark gray stain that marks the underground part of the wall, then broadens out to a crevice toward the bottom of the hole. Maybe I've dug four, maybe four-and-a-half feet. Down the sides of the hole all sorts of trash and stuff pokes out: old bottles and newspaper, a plastic doll's arm, a whole lot of broken up cement. A minute ago I turned over a waxed-cardboard Chinese carry out box like the kind Brenda'd bring home when she was too tired from work to cook.

I swing my feet up over the edge and stand, cracking my back as I stretch. The same thing's going on all over the neighborhood: people excavating, filling in cracks and stopping leaks. The landfill is settling, the foundations shifting. You can see it in the sidewalks where they buckle here and there and in the really old trees, the ones they left standing from before the development, mostly in the alleys: they grow a couple of inches off plumb every couple feet or so, then twist around to keep balance. Basements are flooding. The neighbors swap stories and hunches about the situation over back-yard fences. One guy uses a cement patch, another tries tar. One guy down the street laid a sheet of heavy plastic over the hot tar before he filled in. It lasted a week. The earth is moving under us.

I leave my boots on the porch and go in. My mother is put-ting a plateful of hamburgers on the kitchen table. "Go wash your-self downstairs," she says. "You're too dirty for the bathroom. I just cleaned in there this morning." She turns back to the stove and pushes a pile of onion slices from the cutting board into the frying pan. They sizzle as they hit the grease.

The stairs have a watermark halfway up the second step, maybe a foot off the floor. So does the piano across the room. I smack the keys as I walk by. They rattle and a flat buzzy sound comes out. It's probably ruined, like the couch I wrestled up the stairs and out yesterday so Ma could clean the floor. The couch was Brenda's and I didn't even bother to ask. The city came and took it this morning on their daily round through the neighborhood. In the laundry room I wash all the way up my arms, then splash water on my face, bend-ing low into the laundry tub. I grab a towel from the pile of laundry Ma's left, folded, on the dryer. At least the washer and dryer still work.

"You didn't walk around down there in your stocking feet, now did you?" she calls out before I get to the top of the stairs.

"Yeah, so?"

"So take them off before you come into the kitchen. I just got the floor done in here."

"You just cleaned down there, too. They're clean enough."

"Not for the kitchen, they're not. Go. Take 'em off." I sit on the landing steps and pull off my socks. There's no point in arguing: she woke me up this morning, knocking on the side door with a plastic pail full of cleaning stuff and a mop. I was hung over, squinting at her through the screen door.

"So, what?" she said. "Are you going to let me in or not?" I opened the door.

"Ma, what're you doing here?"

"I'm here to clean." She props the mop in the corner of the landing and sets the pail down beside it. "I'll bet your basement's a mess—not as if *she* ever lifted a finger around the house."

"That's not true."

She pushed past me, into the kitchen and stood, looking around, at the dirty counter, the sink full of dishes. "You're telling me you did all this?"

"Yeah."

"In three days?"

"I been busy."

"Busy." She pushes up her sleeves. "Too busy to finish the work outside when your basement's flooding. I'll give you busy—go get some pants on. I asked Norm Salwoski next door about the basement. He knows just what to do. Go."

I went. Now she's standing over the sink, washing up the cooking things. Lunch is on the table in what looks like every clean dish left in the house: a plate of burgers, a bag of buns and bowls of sliced pickles, onions and tomatoes. She's even put the mustard and ketchup in bowls with spoons in. "It's a lucky thing your gas is still working."

"Ma, sit down. Take a break. You been working all morning."

"So've you. Sit down and I'll be right there." She dries her hands and throws the dishcloth into the sink. "They took the couch?"

"Just about when I got started." I put together a hamburger as she sits down. "There's stuff out all over the neighborhood, these days. With all the rain."

"Rain, hell. Somebody oughta sue the developer—a couple summer thunderstorms and the whole neighborhood floods. Pass me the onions. Norm said he saw a crack outside by his garage this morning. You might ask him if he needs a hand later on."

"Yeah."

"And I emptied the trash," she says with some emphasis.

"Thanks." I pile on the onions and reach for the mustard.

"Empties are heavy, you know."

"*Thanks.*" I pull the bowl of pickles over and nudge a few slices out onto my plate. It's maybe the first solid meal I've had since Brenda left. "I didn't tell Brenda about the couch."

"She didn't tell you about *him*—serves her right." She picks up her hamburger and, both elbows on the table, bites down. Her hands are red from all the soap and stuff, and her wedding ring and the big diamond Dad got her for their fortieth anniversary glitters. She has hands like a woman whose children are all gone: big and raw-boned with nails done once a week. Brenda never did her nails: not professional, she said—just clear polish. And her hands were soft, too.

"So what if she asks?" She takes a napkin from the holder and wipes the corner of her mouth.

"So what? I'll tell her the truth. It got damaged. That's all."

"Serves her right." She glances around the kitchen. The dishes are draining in their rack, the counter top is spotless. It looks like she's even polished the toaster. "Next I'll do the upstairs."

"You got other things to do, ma—don't bother. I can take care of the rest."

"Do I?" She looks up at me, eyebrows raised, over her hamburger. "Since when do you know so much?"

"Look, thanks for everything—really, it's great, but I can take care it."

"*You* got other things to do. God knows—your whole house is coming down around your ears. It could at least be clean."

"Well, okay then. Okay. I'll finish with the hole."

"And talk to Norm Salwoski—he could use a hand, poor man. *His* wife is dead, you know."

Brenda and I married right out of high school, and that's about the whole of it. We both thought she'd finish a business program at the community college before we had kids, but two years turned into three when she transferred to the University commuter campus to finish her degree, and three years turned into five when she went to work. She met the guy in one of her classes her senior year, and they were hired together that spring at an accounting office. Just a coincidence. She'd work a few years, we decided, before we started a family. I was laid off last fall, anyway, and we needed the money. Things just worked out that way.

Outside the sky is clouding over. It *does* smell like rain. Maybe, if I'm lucky, the basement won't flood so bad if I can dig deep enough below the hole. I leave the table and find my socks in the basement, then put my boots on.

Another eight inches down or so I find a man's hat wedged under a chunk of scrap cement. The felt is muddied and cut through by the shovel, but the band still has a feather, mud-colored and clumped together, stuck into it. It's a banker's hat. Or an accountant's. For a moment I turn it over in my hands, feeling the felt spongy and cool. It's the sort of thing a guy's likely to lose: leave behind in a restaurant or on a park bench, maybe in a motel room. The sort of thing a woman sees and picks up and comes running after him with. Maybe she puts it on his head and smiles when she doesn't settle it on quite right. Maybe she kisses him then. I take it by the brim and toss it out of the hole, across the yard. It settles in a heap on the driveway.

"Hey, ain't that litterin'?"

I look up again. Norm is watching from his yard, smiling, leaning on the fence. "They got rules against that, you know."

"Yeah."

"Yeah," he shifts his weight from one foot to the other. "How's it look?"

"Can't tell yet—not down far enough. Good sized hole here, though." I pull myself up out of the dirt, glad for the interruption. I'm maybe five feet down now and the crack still runs straight into the earth. It's probably across the slab, too, for all I know. "Ma said you got the same?"

"Yeah, something by the garage. I noticed the side window broken when I was cuttin' the grass last week—whole wall inside's stressed out of joint." He looks back and spits into his yard, then opens the gate and walks out onto the driveway. "Lucky the roof didn't go." He prods the hat with the toe of his shoe.

"What's this, a hat?"

I look down, following the crack into the dirt. A broken Coke bottle, half full of muddy water, pokes out the side of the hole next to my boot. "Looks like it."

"Jesus. The stuff you come across. Makes you wonder."

"Sure does." I press my heel against the bottle. It slides out of the dirt wall and drops to the bottom of the hole, hitting a chunk of cement with a pop. Bits of glass scatter across the ground, clean on their broken edges, shining like diamonds.

Norm squats down next to me. "Let's see what you got here." He cranes his neck over the edge. "Jesus, that's a bad one. How's things inside?"

"Pretty bad—piano's shot, I guess—but Ma's got things cleaned up now." I hear the water running in the kitchen: the dishes again.

"I saw the couch," he says, like at a funeral. "So Brenda's gone, huh?" I look up. He shrugs. "Your mother told me."

"Oh. Yeah, I guess." It all happened quietly enough, no scenes or arguments out on the lawn or nothing. Just I got home from the hardware store with a new shovel—the old one broke after the first two feet or so, right after the picnic stuff—and her car and a bunch of her clothes was gone. I didn't even bother to go inside, at first. Maybe she was running an errand or something. Maybe I already knew—I don't know how to say it, but two feet down the side of the house, I was catching on. Like from the stuff I was turning up. Maybe we only see things we're meant to notice.

"Well, that's real tough. Oughta know better," he says, standing up again. At first I think he means me. I look up: his head's blocking the sun and rays of light seem to shoot out from around him. He looks like a picture of God in some kid's book—in bermudas and bifocals.

"What?"

"Guys like you got enough troubles. Work an' all that. A wife oughta be a wife. Jesus." He spits into the grass. "We never had that problem—guys my age, you know? We got married for life. Stayed that way."

I look back down. The light around his head's burned into my eyes—I can see it glowing in the bottom of the hole: Norm's halo. "You need any help with the garage, Norm?"

"I don't know. We'll talk later—how's about that?" He's turned away from me and for just a minute, I think that maybe he's crying. Poor guy: the old woman's been dead what—five years? He visits her grave on Sundays. Every Sunday—always with flowers, rain or shine. You see him with a potted plant or a big green waxed paper cone under his arm, walking cross town to the cemetery. You honk the horn and he waves. It's sort of a neighborhood thing. He pulls out a handkerchief and blows his nose, takes a deep breath. "Later. When you're not busy. I'll come over, I'll find you."

"Sure, Norm." I keep my eyes down as he starts back across the yard, then stops at the hat. He gives it another nudge with his foot and grunts to himself. When I hear his screen door slam I get back to work.

The chunk of cement at the bottom of the hole's a big one, a good foot and a half across, and thick—not paving. Part of a building, maybe part of an old house. Part of someone else's basement, from someone else's flood. I work around it for a few minutes, trying to lift it with the shovel wedged under one side, then the other, feeling the handle strain against the weight. It works its way out slowly and the dirt above it on the side of the hole wall falls loose as it swings free. I take a few shovel fulls and toss them up over the top, thinking maybe if I get a good enough clearance around the chunk to get a grip, I can lift it to the edge without help.

I can hear the washer running inside: Ma doing another load of wash—probably rags by now. She's got a system: she works her way down from good clothes to work clothes and finally to towels and then rags. It never changes. Brenda used to think that was funny, the way Ma had rules for everything—like the way she did the dishes with the glasses first, then the plates and silverware and the pots and pans last—but she and Ma never really got along. A minute later the dryer goes on—gotta be towels. Always in the same order. I don't know why—there's probably a good reason. Something you learn over a lifetime's worth of wash.

I'm digging around back behind the chunk of cement when I feel the shovel blade cut into glass: it's a sharp, soft sort of impact, and you can hear the crack of it down in the dirt if you listen. I pull the shovel back and part of a wine glass—the fancy kind with the thin stem and cut designs on the base—falls into the hole. It's just the base and the stem, though: I must've cut it right in half. I aim the blade up, above where the rest of it should be, and dig into the dirt, scooping it out, onto the cement . It rolls out easy, dull and stuffed with dirt, decorated around the bowl with more cut designs. I pick it up.

It's fancy all right: too good to just throw away. I pick up the stem and fit the two pieces together and they almost match, as if the shovel had only cut through and not crushed the glass. The bowl's decorated with a picture of a sailing ship cut into the glass in long thin overlapping lines—real fine stuff, like you sometimes see in gift shops. Maybe engravers do it, I don't know. The ship's a beauty—a whaler or a frigate or whatever they called them: three big high masts with lots of thin ropes cut into the glass, lots of flags and stuff around the sails. A statue of a woman under the bow. It's all detail-work, careful—just beautiful. People pitch out the craziest things. I hold it up: there's a gold line around the edge of the glass at the top.

I turn it upside down on the edge of the hole, on the grass so I won't shatter it, and tap the dirt out. It's full of stiff mud, really, and the stuff sloughs out easy. I rub the bowl of the glass to get the rest of the dirt out, and reach two fingers inside to scrape out what's left. I can hear something scratching around inside and at first I think it's just more glass—a chip or part of something else that got stuck inside—then my finger rubs up against it, and sorta goes inside it, and I pull it out.

It's a ring—an old-fashioned type of thing with lacy open strands of gold wrapping around a stone. I scrape the dirt away from the stone, but it's caked into it all around, so I spit on it and rub the grime away. It's a diamond—or at least something like it, I can see. I pull myself up out of the hole as Ma comes out on the porch again. I hold it up to her.

"Hey, look at this."

"What. What is it?" She bends over the wrought iron rail and squints down at my hand. "It's dirty—what is it?"

"Just a second." I get up and go around to the garden hose on the driveway and turn on the water. The hose coughs a few times and sends up a spray from the nozzle. I hold the ring down into it.

Ma comes around the side of the house. She's got an old sock in one hand. "You aren't hurt, are you? Come inside."

"No. Look." I rub the ring against my jeans and hand it to her. She holds it back and down and squints at it, then dries it off a little more with the sock. "You found this?"

"Inside a wine glass. In the dirt."

She looks up at me, then back at the ring. "Huh. Maybe it's worth something." She hands it back to me. "Have it looked at." She opens the side door and turns to go in. "I'm mending your socks—there's a whole pile of stuff she left in a basket under the ironing board. She didn't have a sewing basket, did she?"

"I don't know." Probably not. I can't remember Brenda ever sewing anything.

"I'm sewing on buttons too, but I have to run out and get some more. I'll be back in a minute." The door closes behind her, then opens again. "You talked to Norm yet?"

"A little while ago. He came over."

"Good." She goes back down the stairs, disappearing into the dark. I take another look at the ring. It's smooth and the stone's clear now—bright in the sun with colored sparks and reflections inside. Maybe it's not real, but it's a good fake. I push it down on my ring finger, but it's too small: it'll just fit around the little finger of my right hand. The front screen door slams. "I'll just be a minute," Ma calls around the side of the house, then her car door shuts and she starts the car and pulls away from the curb, past the end of the drive.

Brenda came back last night for some stuff she said she'd forgot. I was asleep on the couch in the front room when I heard the side door open and the kitchen light went on. The rest of the house was dark and she looked in through the doorway as I looked up.

"What."

She had her hands down at her sides, tense. "I have to get some things."

"Yeah." I go to sit up, lose my balance and sprawl back onto the couch. The room's dark and I can't see the armrest to catch myself. She takes a step past the doorway and the room darkens even more.

"You're drunk, aren't you?"

"Well?" I was—or at least a good part of my way to it. I'd called in to work that morning, saying flu and meaning hangover: I hadn't wasted much time when I'd figured out she was gone.

Brenda turns and goes down the hall to the bedroom. I hear her mutter "Shit," under her breath. The bedroom light goes on and for a few minutes I just lie there, letting my eyes get used to the gloom. She rummages around for a while and then I hear the closet slam and she's back, standing again in the kitchen doorway. "I'm going."

"Yeah, all right." I close my eyes. What does she want me to say—goodbye?

She's halfway out the door before she turns back and, standing in the middle of the kitchen, shouts through the doorway. "You're just a shit, Billy, a drunk shit!"

I kept my eyes closed—too smart for this: I wouldn't give her a scene, won't make her feel as if she's got a reason for leaving besides the guy I guess is in the car outside. I was drunk, maybe, but I'm not about to take the blame. Too easy. Like I wouldn't tell her about the crack in the wall and the water downstairs. It's not her house anymore. When she goes she slams both the kitchen door and then the screen door behind her.

So I spent the second night. The next morning—this morning—Ma was over, bright and early, with a bucket and a bag of groceries.

I go back to the hole. Standing over it it looks much deeper—maybe six feet. As deep as a grave—just about as wide, but not as long. The crack runs in a diagonal from the bottom of a basement window to the dirt I haven't dug out yet, and I don't know how much farther it'll go. Maybe all the way down to the foundations of the house.

The next thing to do is get the cement chunk out of the hole and I think a minute before I pick it up: I'm going to have to lift this almost over my head, then push it away far enough so it won't roll back.

It's a lot to lift at first. I fit my hands around it and feel for a good grip, then hoist it up until I can get a knee under it. It takes all I've got, just about, to hold it there, and I let it rest for a minute, feeling the weight of it push my foot down into the dirt at the bottom of the hole. Above me, with my back against the wall of the house for balance, all I can see is sky above the rim of the hole, and clouds working their way from one side of the edge of the dirt to the other, It's like all we ever see—just our own part of the sky. I get my grip again and brace myself.

I take a deep breath and pull the chunk up to my chest, pressing myself against it to get under it for support. It scrapes against my chin, but I can just hold it if I use all my strength and throw my weight in the right direction. The last thing to do will be to get under it and lift from my knees. If I keep my arms tight and straight, I should be able to throw it over. I look up again to get a feel for the distance, and I'm standing there when I realize I've still got the ring on my finger.

And I don't know why, but I keep my eyes on the ring as I lose my grip, and I'm still looking at it when the chunk drops down and hits my foot and I see stars—real stars, like the sky above me just went out and it's dark. I close my eyes and step back from the chunk of cement, pulling my foot out from under it, and in slow motion, it feels like, I crouch down. For amoment, with my eyes closed, I can see the two of them under the dirt just below me, her glass— the one she just threw her ring into—is missing. They're smiling at each other over the table, holding hands deep below the house, surrounded by every little piece of trash and clue I've dug up. It hurts too much for me to yell out.

I lay my foot against the rock and untie my boot, and every tug on the laces aches until I pull the boot off, and then I see blood coming up through my sock and the real pain hits. Enough to bring tears to my eyes. Enough to make me clench my teeth and shout, because the sky above me is bright, bright day again and the ring is winking on my finger and I'm stuck in this hole, lame and leaning against the crack in the house behind me.

SECRETS OF WOOD

GERALDINE ANN MARSHALL

Hundreds of pine trees stretch in front. Their pitch comforts me as my father's aftershave did when I was a girl. How many times have I hear my father say, "I planted these trees, seedling by precious seedling, while I waited for you to be born."?

How many times did he get up in the night and lead me through those pines so we could hear owls' humming lullabies?

How many times did he hand me a box made of cedar, whose scent only sharpens with fallen time? "Open the lid," he would say as we held the box towards dark air. After the whir of a screech owl or the "Who, who, who cooks for you?" of a barred owl, we would snap the lid shut. "Now, what do you have?"

I would answer, "Owls' lullabies and their secrets of the woods."

Even in the dark, I could see my father's half smile. He would touch the wood, reach into his pocket, pull out a damp rag, smooth little prickles on his box, and say, "Things made of wood are very durable if you take the time to learn the secrets of wood."

Why didn't I ask my father for the secrets? Did he tell me when I wasn't listening? Or did I know his secrets of wood as a child and have forgotten them over years of growing into worlds beyond woods?

I try to meander back into those woods with the father of my childhood so that his life, our life together, is again like those perfectly fitted wooden boxes. But feathers of present griefs, little losses that slip form my father's hands daily, brush—almost as silently as owls' wings but with insistence—against my own hands, keeping me in a present with my father neither of us can mend.

My father can no longer hold a tool steady to make lullaby boxes. He can't remember what a saw is called. My father, who once knew every bird's call, now confuses the screech of a blue jay announcing day with the trembling notes of a screech owl greeting night. My father, who once planted these pine trees seedling by seedling, now loses memory by precious memory.

His hand, the blue veins cold, rests in mine as we walk by daylight through the pines. He steps as a clumsy child might, his boots crunching fallen needles in a slow pattern. I can hear the leather laces flapping and know I should stop and tie them for him, but then he says, "Barbara…," and I know this is going to be a good day. Yesterday, he called me my mother's name, a name he hasn't needed for thirty-eight years.

His good days are sometimes our worst days. I have fallen into ordering for him in restaurants, telling him to put socks on before shoes, asking, "Do you need to go to the bathroom?" On his bad days, he eats what is put in front of him, accepts the socks and shoes, and obediently goes to the bathroom when I close the door. On his good days, he says in a voice that reminds me of the few times he had to insist on my respect as a girl, "I am your father."

When I was a child, my father taught me danger's warning signals: the rattler's first seedy shake, early cracks in a tree that would fall, the rush of a great horned owl's wings. Though tomorrow he will not remember if the day before was a good day or a bad day, I am learning the warning signals of both.

Today I know, as I feel his hand warming from my late pregnancy heat, he can be the parent and I can be the child. He can be the shaman showing me a labyrinth through the woods that will lead to an owl's nest, or a path through the world that will help me become a parent myself.

No degree has taught me how to become a mother, and I am petrified.

"But, Barbara, my fellow scientist, not yet hearing in hearts and bellies the ticking

biological clocks, say, "You're a zoologist. You know this will come naturally."

Have they forgotten studies of chimps that let babies starve, or elephants depending on matriarchal units to get them through motherhood? Perhaps these younger women, all with their own mothers, only paid attention to studies where all does come naturally.

I feel a tremble in my abdomen. My mother who, Aunt Dorcas tells me, was a poet, might have called it quickening. Would my father remember her words for fetal movement? Did they discuss her unpublished poetry before she died? When she was gone, he carried me, a toddler, through these woods while he walked out his grief, while neighbors cleaned the house—and her words were also lost to me. The only words of my mother's that remained were captured on index cards in a yellow recipe box. I keep that plastic box in my lab. The penciling on the cards has faded, but I trace: can mushroom soup, pound hamburger, pinch salt, dash pepper—thinking some mothering poem might be encoded. Now I trace my father's hand, hoping some secret memory is hidden in his mind with its disintegrating neurons, some remembered poem pulsing through brain chemicals no longer connecting in strong paths.

He still is a tall man—my father. He has that round face that refuses to admit age quickly. But his eyes show marks that remind me of bird tracks left in soil given in at last to a persistent force.

Once, he seemed neither young nor old to me, but like the oak tree shading our yard. What else would a child think of the man who was both father and mother?

"Barbara," he says again, his voice a shadow of the baritone that once woke up the woods. His voice makes a pattern of syllables—a pattern that might blow away by tomorrow, in the next hour. "Barbara, do you remember Owlet?"

Until the new drugs no longer lived up to the doctors' promises, and he confused a blue jay's raspy call with a chickadee's buzz, my father kept his rehabilitator's license.

We always had a red-tailed hawk mending in the backyard, a young cedar waxwing spitting blueberries in the living room, or an owl with yellow-green eyes that glowed in the kitchen.

A parade of little girls oohed or yucked through our house. While other kitchens smelled of sweet brownies mothers had made, our kitchen smelled slightly bitter from raw meat: chicken legs, beef hearts, even pink, frozen baby mice that went through the blender to feed young birds.

While other girls learned to sew a hem, I learned to mend a wing. While other girls took ballet, I learned to wear heavy leather gloves, take a bird to the edge of our woods, let it perch before it flew back into the day or night that had let us borrow it for healing. For they all healed, except Owlet.

I was almost grown when I found Owlet. We never named our wildlife charges. Perhaps she was allowed a name because my father's secret wisdom knew she would never return to the wild.

She wasn't actually an owlet, but a full-grown owl, and I was sure a mother. I found her on the road between our house and the college. Was it intuition that had me take the road that morning rather than the bicycle path?

The sun caught her feathers, the broken wing splayed out like pictures I had seen of solar wind in a space only few can reach. I cradled her into my bicycle basket and turned home.

Home was the same house we live in today—the cedar house designed as his first architectural project for the woman who became my mother. She lived in it five years and he has lived in it forty-five, though now I have to draw sock-swaddled feet on the drawers, so that he knows where to find socks. As long as he can recognize symbols and remember the meaning of socks, he can find a path through his own house,

On that day when I was almost grown, one part of my mind kept traveling to the embryology lab where I was supposed to be studying the slides of a chicken embryo. I thought of wing buds, but Owlet had a living wing. Even with purple discoloration I knew was a sign of internal bleeding, I, still with a child's faith, knew my father could heal Owlet.

The rasp of my father clearing his throat brings me back to adulthood. "I couldn't save her," he says.

When I brought Owlet to my father, he filled his hot water bottle and snugged the bird in a box with the red bottle wrapped in towels. I heart the faintest hum as my father bent down to listen to Owlet's chest, but perhaps I only hear my father sighing. "Gurgling," he murmured.

A small bead of bright blood formed at the edge of Owlet's beak. Couldn't we feed her?" I asked. He started to shake his head, but then looked at me. My English professor husband would say it is a cliché to say one can see love in another's eyes, but that is what I saw in my father's eyes—love and pain joining in that one look.

"Do you want to try some milk with syrup?"

I ran to warm the milk with Karo syrup we kept handy for injured birds, and on calm nights, for hot chocolate for ourselves. A moment later, with one hand cupped about the back of her head, I used my other hand to pry open Owlet's beak. I forced my fingers steady and put a medicine dropper of milk into the corner of her beak. I squeezed the dropper, watching the white beads drop uselessly into a soft staining string. She never swallowed my gift of sweet milk.

Then my father's steady hand was covering both my hand and Owlet. "Barbara," he whispered, "I don't think she has the will to stay with us."

Now, my father's hand, with time's tremor no medication will silence, covers my hand again. He guides me until we stop in front of my mother's tree.

The tree is a memory I have been able to touch, even to climb and looked deep into the woods. A maple, for my mother asked for something planted that would change

with the seasons. "I told her," my father says, "we would watch the leaves change together. She touched the top of your head where she had swaddled you to her breast."

He stops. I wonder if he has forgotten this memory, or if there is nothing else to say. He points high into the maple with its spring leaves.

As a girl, it seemed cruel to me that spring would insist on coming after my mother's winter death. I thought this the day my father and I buried Owlet beneath this tree. Spring had already come, but Owlet had left babies in some secret cavity.

"Is my box still there?" my father asks.

I make a mental note to ask about vision side effects from Dad's newest drug, but then realize that I can barely see the nest box in the maze of old branches and new leaves.

My father leans into me as he searches. I feel his beard brush the top of my head. I kept my father clean-shaven, until the day I nicked him. Some days, he rubs the beard and draws his eyebrows together, puzzled at this change in his own face. He though lets the beard pass as a small confusion lost among the larger ones of how to put on his pants and what is the name of that smell he once knew as coffee. Once the baby comes, I do not know if we all be able to live in his house. Will he know she is his grandchild, or will she, like the woman who cares for him when I have to work, be some new shadow he cannot acknowledge?

I have a grant to study memory in birds. How do songbirds incorporate new melodies into old tunes, daily building neural circuits? Does the protein found in zebra finches cause memories to clump together in young finches and lock memories away from old birds? I see the shape of that protein in plaques of human brain tissue. I imagine being able to read that protein as my father once read blueprints, to recreate designs for my father so that he can remember each square foot of his own buildings, know where to add rooms and railings. How do Clark nutcrackers remember the location of seed stores they keep against the cold months? In the caches of my father's mind are there memory stores of my childhood, my mother's face, the language of birds, the ability to make new memories of a grandchild?

Or are there only the memory seeds my father gives me on his best days? I write each in a journal, stored in a box he once made for my treasures of half-moon leavings of robin's shells. I am keeping these gifts for his grandchild. I cannot risk forgetting.

"Barbara, my box is still there!" There are gaps in his smile—he no longer wears his partial plate, but I see my father as he was the day after we buried Owlet.

He greeted me at the door the minute I got home form my classes. "I made it for her." He held up the nest box, cedar gleaming with some secret mixture of oils and lemons that kept birds safe from mites.

How many times did he show me this secret of wood? Too many to count, but I have never gotten that smooth, just-right liquid to glow beneath my stirring spoon. I tried last week to make it with my father, but measurements no longer hold any meaning for him.

But, then, he knew the mysteries of Pythagoras, how to make each angle flow into visible music, how to make each droplet of a solution that made a home safe for birds.

We traveled through the woods and attached the box to my mother's tree, above Owlet's burial ground. I remember my knees scraping the bark through my jeans as I climbed until Dad shouted, "Angle it on the branch." I remember the sound of nails clipping the box to the maple limb, the feel of my father's hammer solid in my hand.

This year, as each year, there is a nest in that box. I am not sure if it is my father humming as he does now in nonsense rhymes of the hum of owlets I hear, but the humming comforts me.

I know now that the nest box is my father's faith box. I was six when he placed, below this very tree, a nicked cedar box in my hands.

"Why," I had asked, "don't we go to church? Mrs. Humphreys says you designed the church, that Mama was a Sunday School teacher."

The next Sunday, we had gone to Sunday School and church and every Sunday after, but when other families went to The Shady Rest Restaurant, we, in all seasons brought a picnic to our woods. In the basket, my father always packed our faith box.

"Your mother and I made this," he told me on our first Sunday picnic, "to hold promises." He looked up at the trees branching above like the beams in the church's ceiling. "In her family, there was always a box on the kitchen table that held Bible verses. She called it a faith box." I opened the box and small cardboard rectangles of verses spilled onto the patches of brown pine needles and maple leaves. I hurried to gather them up, pulling up dry bits of leaves and pine needles, with only a memory of scent still clinging, to make their way with the verses into the faith box.

My father let me pick up each promise on my own, but he held the box steady until I was ready to drop in sturdy red and yellow cards. Those fragments of scripture still make only a puzzle, not an answer, for me.

But, as a child, I knew that it was the act of pulling each card from the box each Sunday and holding it in my hand, feeling its small weight, smelling the cardboard that had absorbed smells of cedar, pine, and Karo syrup—distinctly part of each day's faith—that was important.

I wish now that I had brought the faith box so that he could read me a promise, but I think my father has forgotten how to read. I do not know enough about what he has forgotten, but I know too much about what he will forget. I know he will forget my name, will forget how to swallow, will forget how to breathe.

"Barbara, my box is still there," he says again. I lean against my father, gently, to see the nest box hidden among sheltering leaves. I think I see the cinnamon tufts of a fledgling.

The nest box has weathered and cracked. It no longer gleams, but secrets of wood have given it the strength to hold the future soft singers of these woods until they gain faith to glide on air currents as fragile, as durable, as a dying soul's last or an infant's first grasping breath.

THE CLIPPING

DOLEN PERKINS-VALDEZ

The scrap of newspaper is shaped like an unfamiliar country. The edges are blunt where the paper has snapped off with age. I read it again and again: "ANOTHER NEGRO BURNED. The eyes were burned out and hot irons rolled all over his body. Both testicles were removed before the pleading Negro was set afire." The ones who pick him up promise his wife that there will not be trouble. They are there to protect. He leaves behind a screaming, sobbing woman and two teenage boys whose eyes are haunted with collective memories they have not yet lived. The unstable house leans forward, anxious, as if ready to tumble into the fragmented remains of his past. He never looks back as he follows them. Obediently. Silently.

Curtains drop in neighboring windows as the sound of slamming car doors echo in the street. He is helped into the back of a pickup truck, shouldered between two roughnecks holding rifles and across from a sloe-eyed man holding nothing but anger in his fists. He keeps his eyes on the bed of the truck and jabs his own hands into the pockets of his overalls. Headlights light up the truck as if it is a moving stage. It swings out wide, pitching them to the edge as it turns around in the street. The procession takes its time, two parallel lines of twisted faces flashing gleeful smiles in his direction as they pass. Up, down, up his head bobs along with the truck, a floating ball abandoned in the water.

Octavius Benedict is newly married, having lost his first wife to a disease improperly diagnosed by a veterinarian from neighboring Brownsville. After a year of guilt for not paying the doctor who had graciously offered to come at a reduced fee, a year in which he drank so much that his young sons were forced to grow up fast, a year of waking visions filled with her emaciated, accusing face, he married again to a seditty nurse from Memphis. Perhaps he had been attracted to the fact that she was in a health profession. Or perhaps it was that she believed in him enough to figure that he wouldn't do the same thing to her. She trusted him and the boys trusted her, so he decided within weeks of meeting her to make her his wife.

He makes a living farming another man's land in Bolivar, the boys are back in school now because their newmother insists upon it, and she works as a caretaker for a rich, elderly woman during the daytime. They make do enough to buy a small excuse for a house. Eventually, Octavius falls so deeply in love with this mild-mannered woman that he wonders if his first wife's death was not just a clearing for the second. She even learns how to cook the country way, the way he likes it.

The older son will grow up and move to Memphis. He will marry a high school student he meets there who he will intentionally get pregnant in order to win her over. They will have one girlchild who will use all of her parents' savings to get the education that they didn't.

The younger son will disappear at the age of seventeen after leaving the house one evening for a box of yeast. He will never return, and his newmother will make herself so sick from worry that this time, this loss will kill her as the first one threatened to.

The article about Octavius Benedict's murder will be printed in *The Commercial Appeal.* His wife won't read it, but the older son will cut it out, save it in his birth mother's Bible. He will hold on to it for his daughter after the doctor delivers the news that the infection has gone bad, and his young wife must have her womanly insides removed, depriving him of the sons he so craves. That daughter, my mother, will save it for me, her first son.

That history might be all but forgotten were it not for this clipping, this reminder of a past horrible enough to intentionally erase. I keep it safe, tucked away in a small, private place where I can get to it if I ever need to remind myself of a crisp, autumn night when a man trying desperately to be a man squeezed his wife as he slept, finding temporary peace in a six hour knot of work-worn exhaustion, only to be wakened by a casual knock on the front door.

This is not something our family often speaks of—the only words needed are those on the page, not appended by oral engravings, sketches of heroic endurance, empty libations for someone none of us living can remember.

But my great-grandfather's fortitude is something that those of us on my mother's side who know of it call upon when misfortune strikes. When my grandfather was told that he had the debilitating disease that most likely was what had taken his birth mother, we whispered prayers that blessed the grave of "the one who was killed." When my father was struck by a bus and lay in a coma for two days, the right side of his face decorated with scars, my mother cursed my great-grandfather's attackers and all of the gods that allowed such things to happen. When my childhood cold turned into pneumonia then turned into bronchitis, my mother pressed the clipping to my feverish cheek as if it were an amulet. And when I recovered, she thanked Octavius. My great-grandfather's death is our religion, the clipping our scripture, and the memory our sanctuary.

My mother covets her sons, an unnatural longing that has resulted in my two younger brothers, twins, still occupying the bedrooms of their teens. I am not far off; I live two blocks over in a small, but newish complex in an apartment that my mother decorated. Nine months of the year, I teach first graders at the same school where my brothers and I spent our early, awkward years. Now that it is summer, I spend my days watching television and looking out the window at skinny white girls sleeping by the pool. At night, I talk to people on the Internet, random associations that allow me to change, metamorphose into the faces of my imaginings.

I have read how genes often skip a generation: amber eyes, freckles, complexions, even birthmarks appearing as echoes of ancestors, near and far. I have heard that when a man is hanged, he loses consciousness instantly. But I have also heard that sometimes he doesn't, and he feels his eyes spring out of his head, feels the loss of control of his tongue, feels his neck splitting as he kicks and struggles to summon one more breath.

Even without looking up, he knows which direction he's headed in. He knows every road in this backcountry, even the ones that he never travels. The wind whistles messages in his ear, and he can tell by the odor of the night air that tomorrow it will rain, bringing welcome nourishment to his desperate crops.

He struggles to remember her voice, the voice of the first one who made him feel that he could own the land he worked. Instead, he recalls the musky scent of her womanhood and the way her girlish body filled out until her belly swelled with their love. He remembers how he kissed her newly emerged navel, trailing his tongue around and around it until she exploded in a ticklish fit.

The paved road turns to gravel and then dirt, cloaking them in a battery of dust. It stings his eyes, but he resists the urge to wipe. The truck lurches over dried craters in the road; branches crackle beneath its wheels. Trees flank them on each side, extending their limbs and meeting above like arms embraced, erasing the full moon. Hollering reaches him from the car behind and he knows that they are far enough away from the nearest house that the men can now reveal themselves. Deeper, deeper they go until they reach a glade. Massive clouds edge across the sky, leaving the blink of lonesome stars in their wake. Insects buzz. Trees sway, a chorus of hands rubbing together in anticipation.

The truck stops and the cars form a square around it. Octavius scans the scene in a quick, but thorough survey. Three cars, four men in each. The truck has one in the cab, three in the back. Sixteen total. Too many. They begin to turn out of the cars, some with rifles, others with sticks or broken off broom handles, and one swinging a long, black object that he doesn't recognize in the darkness.

The first son came so easily. The woman who helped birth him said that it was the easiest delivery she'd witnessed in years. In the dark of the kitchen, they'd placed his boy on the piglet scale. 9 pounds even.

The man sitting across from him says, "You the one. You the one done that to Mrs. Wyatt."

Although he says it quietly enough that the others can't hear, Octavius knows that this is the juried pronouncement, the verdict of the vigilante.

He concentrates on the distant chatter of a magpie. And it arouses his memory of her voice. Yes, that's it. He can hear it now. Leaned towards the high register, but incorporated rich, bass notes when she was serious.

The butt of the gun knocks the voice out of his head.

She knows me as "Imtheone." She is simply "Marie." We have been meeting for over a month now, and most of our exchanges have been quick mutual masturbations. She lives with her ex-husband who doesn't know that she can use his computer. He drives a truck most nights. She gets a check.

I know these things because we have begun to talk more, get to know each other. She tells me that her ex is a user and that she fills fake prescriptions under various names. I tell her that I am a twenty-four year old virgin. The screen is blank for a long time after that, and I go fill a glass with orange juice while I await her response.

Marie: Why?
   Imtheone: Why what?
Marie: Why R U still a virgin?
Long pause.
Imtheone: Just cause.
Marie: U never had a girlfriend?
Imtheone: Of course I've had a girlfriend.
Marie: And?
Imtheone: And it just never happened that's all.
Beat.

Marie: My son lost his virginity already.
Imtheone: You have a son?
Marie: He's 12.
Imtheone: I'm sorry.
Marie: Me 2.
Pause.
Imtheone: He's so young.
Marie: It wasn't his fault. She was a little slut.

I don't know why, but I want to end the conversation right now. I worry about seeming rude. Even so, I log off without saying good-bye. She will understand. This is the nature of these things.

The story that the clipping doesn't tell is what actually happened between Octavius Benedict and Wilma Wyatt. Unlike the details of the murder, that part of the history has not been passed down, so I have sketched it in for myself. I imagine that some people reported that Mrs. Wyatt was a low kind of woman and that she and Octavius had a thing going on for some months prior. Others probably said that Octavius bided his time, working for Mr. Wyatt for all those years and watching the old man's wife through the back window of the house nearest the field where he and the others grew wheat. And they probably said that when that conniving bastard finally got the chance, he took it. And maybe there were others in the town, the publicly silent few who whispered behind doors and windows that Octavius was too in love with both of his women to have a lustful eye for a middle-aged shrew like Wilma Wyatt.

This is what I think of after the conversation with "Marie." I sleep dreamlessly, but I wake up to the same thoughts of the night before.

He manages to respond to the command by pushing himself off the ground to a stand. When everything slows, he observes the man before him, a face that he knows, recognizes from the feed store. The obvious leader. Other faces, too, recall scenes, reminders of something that now feels distant. But there is no mutual acknowledgement. The transformation has happened. These men are now remnants of the selves they occupy outside of this secret space, closeted by trees so thick that it seems as if there is no yesterday, no tomorrow. If he strains, Octavius can hear their rapid, uncontrolled breathing over the quieting wind. Their bodies flex with desire.

"Don't you have nothing to say? An explanation for your cowardly act."

Octavius waits without speaking. He will not give them that benefit. He will not arouse them further.

The man looks past him, and Octavius cannot suppress the urge to turn around. He had not noticed it before, but there is one tree near the edge of the circle with a single, lone branch jutting in his direction, like a finger pointing. A long, thick thing dangles from it in an ominous curl.

Both of his sons had been easy births. He feels good about the older one because he is strong. Bull-headed, but cool. He knows how to keep his temper in check. It's the younger one that he worries most about. He's only thirteen, but Octavius can already tell that he will not fare well in this world. The boy doesn't understand because of his immaturity, but he refuses because of his independence. Like the time that Octavius told him not to be taking that shortcut through Donnie Pryor's field. And then the whipping he'd had to stand by and watch the old man give his boy when he was caught. Or the time when their cat was found cut open wide, and the little one, barely of school age, convinced that he knew the culprit, had thrown a rock at the suspected offender's dog, leaving the mongrel with a crooked, sideways walk and one eye running from the other. The determined lip of that boy was enough to kill him. Octavius wonders if he should have beat him more. He'd never laid a hand on either one of his boys, and now he wonders if he should have. Thinking of this grieves him.

Someone kicksweeps him and he collapses. The follow-up kick in his ribs knocks the wind out of him.

"You think you can just have any white woman you want, don't you. You think you can just stick your thing in any of our women anytime you get ready, don't you."

The voices run into one another, as if it is only one person speaking. They kick him in the stomach, the back, and put a boot to his neck. He tries to protect himself by cradling his head. But it leaves other parts exposed and they swing at him with their homemade weapons, weapons easily disposed of in a backyard bonfire. One of his eyes pulsates and it goes dark on that side.

"Teach…you…we'll…teach you."

They drag him by his feet, and the ground burns his back, scraping the skin. Unconsciousness threatens, but he fights it. He cannot think, can only react instinctively in a litany of Jesuses in his head. Then even the words stop, and he is reduced to that which they make him.

It's the twins' birthday, and my mother is planning the type of party that you'd give a child. Foil balloons float around the house, and I can hear the rustle of wrapping paper coming from her closed bedroom door. My father has been standing over the grill all morning, flipping slabs of ribs, foot tapping to Bobby Womack, wet runny face grinning through the smoke. He is holding court with our neighbor, another man his age reliving his bad motherfucker past and getting badder the more beers they have.

The twins are upstairs competing, so concentrated on their video game that their mouths make strange, grimacing movements as they maneuver gun-toting characters around the television screen with their control pads. They barely look up when I greet them with a "wassup" from the doorway. I envy the nonchalance of their manhood.

The sprawling house feels empty to me. An impersonal box. I wander through the oversized rooms, seeking a place where I can camp out, remain unobserved. My mother views the size of the house as a tribute to the triumph of our family. I see the house as repressive, confining.

I dread meeting with the usual crowd, my parents' circle of overly affectionate friends who will endlessly remark on how big the twins have gotten and how they are still as identical as ever, as if they can think of nothing more interesting to say to two college dropouts. Then they will ask me about school and how they think male elementary school teachers are darling and when will I have one of my own. Later, after the twins have devoured as much meat as they can, run thoughtlessly through their gifts, after they have taken a swim in which they race each other until they are bronzed and breathless, their friends will arrive hours late to the party and they will all leave without telling anyone. This will happen just as my parents and their loud-talking bunch bring the party inside and set up a card table.

The muffled sounds of partying seep through the closed door of my bedroom-turned-home office. The screensaver on the computer monitor is no doubt my mother's idea, an African mask with an elongated face and high regal forehead. I log in as "SweetWillie" and become a lurker, watching bits of conversations play out in public chatrooms, people struggling to connect amidst a myriad of voices so that they can later Instant Message one another in private.

"Hey you."

I jump and turn around, instinctively pushing the button that will close my active window, revealing a website for a popular news-magazine. It is the fluid motion of one who is practiced enough to always be prepared to hide his computer activities.

"Hey," I say. I know her. She is the daughter of that Judge, what-shisface. We went to high school together. I remember that her name is Salina. I remember that she had a certain reputation.

"Your mom told me you were probably back here. I'm bored out there."

"Oh."

"I can come in, right?"

"Sure." I fumble for a moment as she pushes the door open. Even though it is now an office, I still feel territorial about it as if it is still my bedroom. She sits on the wine-colored loveseat, and drapes an arm across the back. The room fills with her presence, and her eyes refuse to give me a moment's relief.

"You look the same," I say. This is my attempt to say that she looks good. Pretty. Sexy. Dangerous. She still wears the same short natural she wore in high school. But her outfit is grown up, modest, loose-fitting. Even so, I can make out her curves because she is plumper than she used to be. It is hard to hide so much thigh, so much breast.

I catch her eye and she appears to be watching my mouth, as if she expects me to be on the verge of saying something important. I sit suspended between her and the computer screen, frozen in utter inadequacy.

"You look good. Better." She nods at the screen. "What were you doing?"

"What?"

"There." She points at the screen.

"Nothing. Just…surfing."

She stands and walks towards me. I am transfixed by her jiggles. She leans over me and takes the mouse beneath her fingertips. Something grazes my cheek. I stiffen.

"Let me show you something," she says. She types in an address that I cannot see past her bulk.

She stands back. Able to breathe again, I wait as the website comes up. It's her personal homepage. SALINA scrolls across the top above an image of her, an image that is different somehow from the Salina standing before me.

"Do you like it?"

"Why do you have a homepage?" I ask.

"I want to be an actress. This website is for my publicity shots. Look at them. You're not even looking at them."

"In Memphis? How are you going to be an actress in Memphis?"

"Why not? You can act in Memphis. You're not looking." She clicks on her face.

"But why not move to L.A.? That's where you need to go."

A picture of her wearing an orange bikini comes up on the screen. Then it fades into another picture, in a different bathing suit. Picture after picture of a near-naked Salina.

"Because I'm good enough to make it here." She melts into my neck.

My body responds without my telling it to. My arm girdles her waist. I pull her to me until she is sitting on my lap, and I am surprised by the confidence of my touch. I am now "SlickWillie" and she is the temptress of her pictures. We lean back in the office chair, as far back as it can go. She takes my face in her hands and says "it's okay, it's okay" over and over, as if she is granting me permission. I rub her against me.

"Honey?"

Salina nearly falls out of my lap in her haste to get up. My mother wobbles in the doorway, her eyes small and red.

"What are you two kids doing back here?" Her words slur and she spills some of her drink on the rug. "Honey, I need to talk to you. Salina, please excuse us, please excuse us for a minute. Would you baby? Would you do that for me?"

I smooth the front of my pants over and over. Salina exits without a word, without even a glance in my direction. The looping slide-show of her in bathing suits continues to run on the screen. But my mother is in no condition to notice.

"You need to go to bed."

"Boy, please. I've just had a few drinks, that's all."

I lead her over to the couch and take her drink from her before she spills the remainder of it. I place it on the table.

Then she stops me with her words. "I need the clipping."

Her eyes shutter as if she is straining to stay awake. And I know what is to come before I even ask.

"Why?"

"Because I'm giving it to your brothers for their birthday. None of that other shit meant anything to them. I'm going to give them something that means...you know...something that means...something. You know."

I back away, hating her. I want to slap her.

"No, Mama."

"You still got it, don't you? You still got the clipping?" The side of her face jumps and the slur now carries the heavy southern drawl of her youth, a secret that she only shares on special occasions.

I back out of the door and run down the stairs. As I turn the corner, I walk right into a soft mass of flesh. Salina presses herself against me. "Is your mom sleep yet? I figured she came upstairs to take a nap."

She has me cornered, and I feel my control slipping, my heat rising. I begin to hyperventilate. Her eyes glint sinister in the dark of the hallway.

I push past her and run out the back door. The sound of glasses clinking and B.B. King picking the guitar grows fainter behind me as I run, run past the pool through the grass, hurdling over fences, away from the house, away from my apartment, away from my shame.

He is running, pushing through tangles of trees and brush. His sense of direction is completely gone, but he thinks he knows enough not to circle back. And the animals are helping. He can hear the ripping shouts of the men behind him, the firing of their rifles as they mistake the movement of night creatures for him.

Got. To. Get. To. Her. And. Them.

His thoughts come back as one-syllable words. He has just come as close to death as any man ever has, but he still thinks only of them. He can no longer feel the raw wounds of his seared flesh, the broken fingers, the torn rectum, his mind broken into enough pieces to tell him to fight through sixteen men, grab the hot iron, swing it at one of them so hard that he could hear the skull crack, and run into the trees.

And the woods welcome him, brambles grazing him gently as if refusing to hurt him any more than he has already been hurt. A strange bird follows him overhead, directing him as it flits from tree to tree. On the ground, a spry raccoon hurries him along, turning to look at him as if to say "keep up." His breath comes in rapid gusts, but he is not winded. He feels as if he can run forever.

The. Boys. The. Boys.

Up ahead, he can see the light of a house. His house. The bird cheers him along, congratulating him on his success, and the raccoon reminds him that his pursuers aren't far behind. He is almost there. She will know what to do. She will have the rifle and she will kill as many as she can. She will help. She will know what to do.

He sees the man and the woman before they see him. The man is standing on his porch in his underwear, peering into the forest. She is illuminated in the doorway, a vision in white.

"Who's out there?" the man calls.

The calls of the posse behind Octavius grow louder and more distinct. They are no longer wasting ammunition by shooting aimlessly into the dark, but the man on the porch seems to sense that there is danger coming. He goes into the house and returns with a gun, shoving the woman inside.

The bird urges Octavius on and he runs out of the darkness into the man's line of sight.

"Help. Me."

He believes that he feels the burning sensation in his shoulder before he hears the sound of the gun. But he keeps going in the direction of the man and the warm glow of the house.

"Get back, now. Get back off my property." He cocks his rifle.

Octavius slows, but keeps walking.

The gun cracks again and Octavius feels the pain surge through his leg. He falls to the ground, clutching his knee, crying for the first time that night.

Just before the posse reaches him, Octavius looks up and sees the man pull the white-faced woman away from the window. She looks right down at him, and he is close enough to the house to believe that he sees pity in her eyes. The lights in the house dim.

This time, as they drag him back into the woods, rougher and angrier than before, Octavius cannot even remember who he is. And he wonders how he got there.

THE HEATSEEKER

MICHAEL SCHIAVONE

Jake's nodding off to his 4:30 appointment: a seventeen year old girl who does a U-turn when she's supposed to do a three point; who fails to stop at the J. Edgar Hoover Elementary School crosswalk; who doesn't yield to oncoming traffic as she turns left onto the Embarcadero. But, all the same, she keeps her hands on the steering wheel at all times. Back in the parking lot, Jake signs her test card, permitting her to operate a motor vehicle in the state of California.

He skirts through the first floor crowd of the Department of Motor Vehicles (license renewals, out-of-state transfers), making his way to payroll. They owe him overtime for working Marla's shift, who's been battling her ex-husband in court. Jake heard from his friend Lucy in duplicate registrations that Marla's ex broke into her apartment and spray painted the kitchen orange, everything from the toaster to the tea pot. This story made Jake feel better about his own relationship with Donna.

Jake pulls into the loose gravel driveway and sees a green Datsun with New Mexico plates. He parks next to the strange car, shutting down the engine. Outside, he peeks into the driver's side window. There's a stuffed, brown Burger King bag, a road atlas, and an empty bottle of Arizona Iced Tea on the dashboard. Jake takes a tire iron from his trunk. Stopping before his entrance, he swings the iron at invisible assailants. When he presses his ear against the cold door, he hears the ridiculing sound of women's laughter. He keys open the door.

Donna's sitting on the radiator in Jake's bathrobe, a plastic pink cup in her hand. A girl is sitting Indian style on the floor, sipping a bottle of A&W through a bendy straw. In her left hand she holds The Mosquito, a small, blue rocket Jake put together a few weeks ago. Donna shoots up from the radiator, juice spilling over the side of her cup.

"Jake, honey," she says, tugging on his arm. "I want you to meet my daughter, Crystal."

Crystal rises slowly from the floor. "I like your rockets," she says, holding up The Mosquito. A pot belly pushes through her sweat-shirt. Her hair is a short, unnatural red. Jake keeps his eyes fixed on The Mosquito.

"Crystal's going to be staying with us for a few nights. She's on her way to...where'd you say you were going to, Crystal?" Donna asks, face crunched in confusion.

"Eureka," she says, rubbing the rocket's tail a bit too hard with her index finger.

"Eureka," Donna repeats.

"What's in Eureka?" Jake asks..

"My boyfriend, Tommy. He's working on an organic farm up there and we're going to live with him." Crystal returns The Mosquito to the bookshelf with the others and Jake lets out a breath.

"She's three months in, Jake. Can you believe it?" Donna asks. "My own flesh and blood is about to have her own flesh and blood."

That night, Jake pulls out the bed from inside the couch. While Donna's in the bath, he lays out a down comforter, a torn sleeping bag, and his pillow from the bedroom.

"I'm sorry I don't have better arrangements for you," he says to Crystal. "I'm not used to overnight guests and I didn't know you were coming."

Jake sits down on the radiator. Crystal sorts through her flowered suitcase.

"We're okay," she replies. "This is just fine. We've been through worse," she says, rubbing her belly.

"You've been living in New Mexico?"

"Yeah, at my cousin Tate's place. I've been waiting around for Tommy to get set up in Eureka. Now he's ready to have us."

"Sounds all right," Jake says.

Crystal lies back and thumbs through a worn Dr. Spock baby book. Jake gets up from the radiator and walks to the kitchen. He unwraps three cube steak filets and reaches for a beer. While the steaks sizzle in butter, he imagines he's cooking dinner for a family.

Jake makes up a plate for Crystal, lightly salting the instant mashed potatoes, cutting the steak into small squares. Figuring an expectant mother should have her greens, Jake digs through the freezer for vegetables, but there's only ice cream and Eggos, so he slices up a tomato instead. He pours a glass of milk and brings Crystal her dinner.

The Dr. Spock baby book rests on her chest, rising and falling with her sleeping breath. Jake shuts off the television. In the kitchen, he wraps Crystal's meal in foil and then sticks a post-it note on the cover of her book, telling her about dinner in the fridge should she get hungry. He glances at The Mosquito on the bookshelf, ensuring it's okay as he makes his way back to the kitchen. Standing above the kitchen counter, Jake eats his steak.

In the bedroom, Donna sips a gin and ginger while fanning her wet, red toenails.

"I left you some dinner in the fridge," Jake says, pealing off his undershirt. "Crystal's gone to sleep."

"Thanks, hon. I'm not just hungry yet, though."

He creeps into bed and leafs through a manual for his new rocket, The Wizard, which he plans on starting in the morning.

"So, what do you think of Crystal?" Donna asks.

"I like her fine. I didn't know you had a daughter."

"I gave her up for adoption and she looked me up about five years ago. We've had lunch a few times when she's been in Sante Fe. Nineteen and she seems to have her life together. That's pretty

MICHAEL SCHIAVONE   99

good." Donna sits up and takes a considerate drag from her cigarette. "If I'd have known her longer, it'd be different. There'd be more between us."

"I think I should know stuff like this, Don. We live together. That's how these things are supposed to work."

"I'm sorry, hon. I didn't think it mattered much." She leans over and pecks his cheek. "You starting a new one tomorrow?" she asks, pointing at the rocket manual on his lap.

"Yeah. The Wizard."

"That's a nice name for a rocket." Donna shuts the lamp on her side. "Goodnight, hon."

Jake lies back and massages his forehead.

He had met Donna at the Oakland-Alameda Annual Pig Roast. After five pork sandwiches and a six pack of Ballantine Ale, Jake ambled to the parking lot and went to sleep in the back seat of his car. He would have slept through the night had Donna not backed her Brat into his car door.

"Shit, mister. I'm sorry," she said, knocking on the back window. "You're okay, right? Everything's okay, right?"

"Yeah, I'm okay," Jake said, rolling down the window. She had short, frantic black hair.

"Your car has a scratch is all," she said, nodding. "Any way we can keep this between us seeing as I'm a bit bombed? The pig roast and all."

"It's okay," Jake said. "Let's just forget it."

"Well, that's real sweet of you. Name's Donna," she said, extending her hand. "How about I take you out for breakfast?"

"Sounds all right," Jake said. "I'll drive."

At Sal's Diner in Oakland, Donna told him how she moved to California a year ago from New Mexico where she had lived all thirty-five years of her life. She said she worked at the Filthy Oyster on Market and 6th, but the tips were lousy. Donna told him how she'd really like to be an actress, that she had a lot of drama to offer. Jake paid for breakfast and lent her twenty dollars since she was cashed out. Back in his car, she pulled the napkin dispenser from the breakfast table out of her backpack.

"Here," she said, placing it on the dashboard. "I got one in my car. Comes in handy."

Jake stopped by the Filthy Oyster a few nights later. When Donna saw him, she brought him a Bud bottle, telling him to sit tight until she got off at seven. He played pinball in the corner, watching her between games, admiring her movement. She carried six glasses of beer without a tray, whistled to the white haired bartender when she needed another round, patted the men's backs when she delivered their drinks. After Donna's shift, they went to Abe's Place. They danced to Rolling Stone covers wailing from the mouth of Abe Jr., the owner's son. Jake dipped Donna to *Angie*, spun her to *Street Fighting Man*. Then she kissed him during *Under My Thumb*. Back at Jake's place, they drank gin and gingers through straws.

"What are these rockets about?" Donna had asked, pointing toward his collection on the oak bookshelf.

"My hobby," he replied. "Been building them since I was a kid. My dad and I would launch them on Sundays."

"How do they work?"

"Well," Jake said, cradling The Silver Fox in his hands. "A parachute will come out from here," he said, pointing the straw in his mouth toward the rocket's belly. "Sometimes they'd blow off course and we'd lose them. I hated that."

"You don't launch them anymore?"

"No. They're for display now. Like models."

"That's cute," Donna said, gently pinching his nose. He could smell cigarettes on her fingertips. She then took The Silver Fox from his hand, returned it to its place on the bookshelf and led him to his bedroom.

"So, how do you go about becoming an actress?" Jake asked, handing her an empty Coke can so she could smoke in his bed.

"Auditions in San Fran."

"You tried any yet?"

"Not yet," she said, examining the backs of her hands. "I haven't found the right roles. It has to be something that suits me. Like a lady detective or a vigilante. I don't want to be some flunky in the background."

Jake didn't know much about acting, but he figured you had to be a flunky before you could be a vigilante. He knew, for example, that it took him a year at the DMV before he was allowed to process vanity plate orders. He didn't press her about it, though. Maybe she could make it without the toil.

Jake wakes at six. The rocket manual is still in his hand. In the kitchen, he puts on a pot of coffee and rubs his eyes awake. Crystal's asleep in the living room. The coffee mug warms his fingers as he walks into the garage and sits down at his desk. It's not really a garage since it can't fit Jake's Grand Marquis, but it's an ideal workshop. The Wizard is a skill level 2 rocket which means it'll be a snap for Jake who typically constructs skill level 4 models. Jake bought The Wizard because it has two parachute ducts, which is rare.

Rubber cement hardens on his fingertips as he glues the fins to the rocket's tail. He blows on the base of the wings, the glue barely visible on the rocket's shaft. Jake will have to wait several hours before applying paint and decals.

A timid knock comes from the other side of the door.

"Come in," Jake calls. Crystal opens the door and peeks in.

"I just wanted to thank you for the steak. It turned out to be breakfast instead of dinner."

"It's all right. You can come on in if you feel like it," he says, pulling a paint stained stool next to him. "Don't worry. The paint's not wet."

Crystal takes a seat on the stool and rubs her hands together. Her big toe sticks out of the hole in her sock. "Is this the new one?" she asks, pointing at the rocket.

"It's called The Wizard. It'll be purple when it's done."

"Donna says you don't launch them. How come?"

"No reason, really. It's something I used to do with my dad when I was a kid. After he died, there wasn't anyone around to launch them with. Simple as that."

"I think it'd be cool to see them fly. Donna says they have parachutes inside of them."

Jake nods. He finds it a bit unsettling that Donna and Crystal spoke about his rockets while he wasn't there. He can't imagine why either one of them would care if they flew or not. Maybe that's all they had to talk about, though. There isn't much else to look at in his place. Few women had asked him about his rockets. And not one had ever cared to ask how they work, like Donna did. He knew that wouldn't count much to some people, but that's what he tried to think about when he thought about Donna.

"Well, I'd sure like to see those rockets fly," Crystal continues.

"What's that?" Jake asks, shaking Donna from his brain.

"I said I'd like to see a launch."

"I'd have to buy some engines."

"Are they expensive?" Crystal asks. "I mean, if they're expensive, then forget it. I just thought—"

"—It's a good idea. You should see something more than me and Donna while you're here."

Inside, Jake gives Crystal snow pants, a ski hat, and a thick pair of wool socks. Donna cuts a head hole in a black Glad trash bag. "This'll be my poncho," she says. Rain falls lightly and Jake can hear the wind whipping against the hanging birdhouse outside the kitchen window as he thinks about which rocket to bring. Sorting through them, he decides on The Heatseeker since it's fire engine red, making it easier to spot in the air.

In the back seat of the car, Crystal studies the instruction manual for The Heatseeker while Jake's inside at Hal's Hobby Shop buying an engine. Donna's applying lipstick in the vanity mirror, puckering in between strokes. Jake bangs on the back of the window which makes Donna and Crystal jump. He holds up the engine in his right hand before getting back inside the car.

"That's the size of a small candle," Crystal says. "I thought it'd be bigger."

"It's no car engine. They're more like little firecrackers." He hands Crystal the engine.

"Well, I think it's cute," Donna says, rubbing Jake's rain soaked shoulder. "Where we gonna launch it?"

"Hillhouse High's football field. All the open spaces I used to know are now strip malls."

Jake drives carefully on the slick roads, aware that he has a pregnant child in the back seat. He notices that Donna and Crystal have the same fingers: slim, long, and sharp. He looks at his own hands which belong to him alone.

At Hillhouse High, they walk toward the center of the football field where a faded white eagle is painted onto the grass. Donna holds The Heatseeker under her trash bag poncho, protecting it from the rain. Crystal keeps the manual and engine in her pants pocket. Jake has Donna's Jack Daniels lighter tucked into his sock. Their boots make sucking noises as they trudge through the thick mud of the field. Jake sneezes and Donna hands him the bandanna she had tied around her wrist. When they arrive at the eagle, they stop. The sky is the color of clay.

"It's gonna be hard to keep an eye on the rocket in this sky," Jake says, tearing grass from the ground, forming a small, dirt circle. "The parachute's yellow and it's a lot bigger than the rocket, so keep an eye out for that."

Donna kneels and pulls The Heatseeker out from underneath her poncho.

"Good job keeping it dry, Don," Jake says to her.

Crystal hands him the engine.

"Thanks, Crystal. You sure you should be out here in this weather?"

She nods yes.

"Now you girls stand back behind me. Sometimes these things go haywire when they blast off."

Jake inserts the B4-2 engine into the rocket's tail. He takes two strips of recovery wadding and jams them inside the shaft, surrounding the engine in order to avoid body damage after takeoff. Then he sets the igniter and plug.

"Ready, girls?"

"Ready," they say at the same time.

Jake gets a good flame going on the lighter and moves the fire slowly toward the engine wick, keeping his face as far away from the rocket as possible. Through the wind and rain he hears the sharp hiss of ignition and rolls away from the launch pad, knocking into the girls' shins behind him. The Heatseeker blasts off.

"Holy shit!" Donna shouts.

Jake looks up, but all he sees is a gray, cloudless sky. "Where is it?"

"It's way above the end zone," Crystal says, slapping Jake's shoulder.

"I still don't see it," he says.

"It's going past the end zone now," Donna says. "The wind's carrying it toward the woods."

Jake forms a visor across his forehead with his hands. "I can't see it."

"Let's just wait for the parachute," Crystal says.

Donna takes Jake's hand while they wait. Rain beads on her black trash bag poncho. Crystal twists her boot into the mud. The rain comes at them sideways as the wind picks up. A tugboat horn sounds from the distant bay.

"I see it!" Donna shouts. "It's gonna land in the woods," she says, jumping and pointing. "I see the yellow parachute."

Jake still can't see it.

"I don't see it," Crystal says.

"You guys stay here," Donna says. Her black bangs are wet over her eyes. "We're not going to lose this one."

Donna runs to the end zone and then cuts left toward the woods. With this wind, Jake figures The Heatseeker is halfway to Sacramento, but he won't dare halt Donna's pursuit.

"This was a dumb idea," Crystal says. "I'm sorry, Jake."

Jake keeps his eyes fixed on his girlfriend as she chases The Heatseeker through the thick, gray afternoon.

"We'll try it again another time, Crystal. You get back to the warmth of the car," he says, handing her the keys. "I'm going to see about Donna."

SURGE

ERIN SOROS

The bus windows rattled with the engine starting as Olaf plunked down next to his sister. The leather smelled like an old man. All the big boys sat together in the back of the school bus where they were shouting now about how they were going to climb the surge tank all the way to the top, this time they wouldn't turn chicken and creep back down. They called at Olaf, laughing and tossing a roll of caps toward his head. He pretended he couldn't hear. Pulled at the collar of his shirt, the fabric scratching his neck, and then opened his book to stare at the lines of black on white. The bus was a cage full of noise. Greta stretched over his shoulder to look back at the boys, but Olaf knew they'd be talking too fast for her to read their lips.

She slipped back into the seat. Each time the bus rounded a corner, her hip dug into his thigh.

He turned to face her, stretching his lips into huge ugly shapes. "What did you do at school today, Greta?" he asked, exaggerating each word. Before she could respond he began to sign. This time he wasn't making words. He was fluttering his fingers as fast as the wings of an insect. Greta stopped rocking her legs. Her mouth formed a small knot.

"It's a bee," he said, his voice warmer now, as if he'd been waiting all along to share this trick with his sister. "Just a bee. See Greta? The letter *B*." He pinched her under the arm until she squealed and pulled away. She giggled. Even her laugh sounded wrong.

The bus dropped off most of the children, who lived near town. Only Ralph was left. The bus creaked and huffed up a hill and around the next bend. When it braked, its metal joints complaining, Ralph walked to the front, nodded once goodbye, then was gone. The bus rocked over gullies and bumps, Olaf and Greta its only passengers. They sat with their hands in their laps, surrounded by rows of green seats. Olaf stared out the window. Instead of sky, he saw hemlock and spruce, cedar and fir, the glass cloudy with Greta's breath so the trees were smeared into an unbroken green wall. *Skirt tree*, Olaf signed in his lap as they passed the giant red cedar that marked the halfway point to home, its base stretching out like the sweep of a lady's skirt. His hands took the shape of what passed: the abandoned truck, the white pine burned black by lightning, the break in the woods that showed a slice of ocean, the pile of rocks where Greta scarred her knee. Each landmark he signed and Greta matched his sign.

Behind these trees, closer to the shore, were the houses the Japanese families had been forced to leave behind. Greta liked to ask him what was inside—beds and tables, like their own house? But Olaf didn't want to imagine the rooms, each one dim as a shadow. Beside the busy stink of the mill town, beside their own lives in the boisterous logging camp he knew so well, the woods were full of people who were gone. From here no one could see the empty buildings, but he still felt uneasy whenever he passed this part of the road, as if the houses themselves were what made the families disappear.

Before the children were taken away, Greta had given one of the boys a ball of red yarn, just like that, something she'd stolen from home. What would he need yarn for, Olaf had asked her—a boy? He had held it tenderly, away from his body, the way one would balance a bomb. Olaf remembered his cupped hands, the knuckly fingers that were calloused from fishing like a man's would be, but sweaty and dirty from run-sheep-run.

Greta did those kinds of things. She did it without thinking about who was the enemy.

Now Olaf didn't sign their word for house. He looked up the road to find something else he could name.

The road narrowed and branches scratched at the windows, trying to speak. Greta leaned her head on his shoulder. They rode higher for three miles, the trees coming closer, the road darker. Then the bus stopped, and they climbed out. The driver told him to look after the little girl.

No buildings here, just the dirt road splitting the forest in two and the scrub where they hid their bikes. The logging camp was four miles farther, up the mountain on a road too steep and rough for the school bus, a single lane used for empty trucks heading up and loaded trucks heading down, the vehicles blasting warnings with their air horns at each bend in the road. The children pushed their bikes a bit, then got on to pedal, Olaf listening for oncoming trucks.

In the summertime, they stopped for huckleberries, squirting them between their teeth. They would sit at the crib dam and spit the sour ones into the tumbling water. But today the air bit their knuckles. He needed to get Greta home. He tried to yank his sleeves down over his wrists. Greta followed him a few yards back, moaning at the wind. When they reached the hill, she climbed off her bike to walk.

"I'm not walking with you," Olaf twisted around to say. "You've got to pedal." He kept his grip tight.

She propped the bike against her hip so she could sign that she was tired.

"Keep going," he said. "Get back on."

He was not going to get off to push both their bikes, not this time. There was nothing wrong with her arms.

All the way to the crib dam she trailed behind him, walking her bike with one hand, the frame leaning so far to the right that Olaf thought it would tip. He pedalled as slowly as he could. His bike rocked side to side, and he had to keep dropping one foot to the ground to keep it steady.

"It's getting dark!" he shouted, turning back to her, not sure if she could see his lips in the dusk. Soon they wouldn't be able to talk at all.

He crossed the crib dam—the wide concrete buttress smooth under his tires, the water clamouring far below—then stopped to let her catch up. He ducked into the bush. She trudged along. When she passed him, she didn't look up, just kept her gaze on the slow spin of her bicycle's wheel.

She turned the bend. Then he was pedalling back down the logging road, away from her, his legs spinning as furious as the sound of the water. He would be at the bottom of the hill by the time she turned around to look. The bike picked up momentum as the wheels skidded over pebbles that flew into the brush. He was not going to be able to stop. He was going too fast for the brakes to work and he'd spin into whatever truck was coming his way. He soared past the last clump of trees, then with a quick shove he let the bike go free from under his body, the metal clanging and the handlebars twisting as he dove and landed on his chest.

His lungs clenched. Nothing. He gasped. A rush of breath. He rested his lips and forehead on the cold damp earth and felt his wind return.

He rolled over, and sat with his knees up, brushing the rocks and dirt from his trousers. He shook his feet. Not even a twisted ankle. Trembling he got up to check the bike, tapped his boot against the tire, then straddled the frame to twist the handlebars into place. He got on, moving slowly to test it, then faster, down the main road that led back to town. He wondered if Greta had got home already.

When he reached the dirt bank, he found a tangle of bikes where the boys had tossed them aside. The twilight made the chrome glisten, a clump of metal bones. He dragged his bike up the bank and dropped it on top of the pile.

The surge tank was another mile down the trail. Only one boy had ever climbed it. Now that boy was fighting in the war.

Olaf ran into the trail that led to the beach. He could see the tank, the metal tower rising three-hundred feet. Under the darkening clouds it was whiter than usual. He hurried, angry at the brambles and branches, stopping to catch his breath when he finally pushed through the end of the trail where it opened onto the beach. Even in the dusk he knew to tell apart the brown and blue and green shapes of this coast, the tides pulling the waves away, the waves grasping at scattered driftwood as though this flotsam could hold the water to the shore. A log boom roofed the left side of the bay. There were more logs scattered on the beach: along the rocky sand the logs formed a jagged alphabet, jammed end to end or criss-crossed, chewed almost hollow by torritoes. Boulders and stumps bordered the miles and miles of trees, the stink of kelp vying with the sharp pine oil.

Down by the boom the boys were tossing rocks into the ocean, not skipping them—just lobbing handfuls of rocks into the air and letting them drop. The boys made bombing sounds.

"Hey," Olaf called out.

The five opened up their circle to let him stand with them. He picked up a rock and tossed it into the water. Waves reached up and closed around it.

"Let's go," said Joel. The boys scrambled up the beach single file, each kicking rocks ahead, trying to hit the nearest boy in front.

Ralph stopped when he found a good flat stone, and they all waited for him to skip it. They counted as it bounced off the smooth water.

"Nine," Karl said, and whistled. They started walking again, crunch of mussel shells under their soles, none of them willing to try to beat Ralph. Olaf slipped his boots into the others' footprints, his face hot against the cold air. He could see the surge tank clearly now. The white paint glowed like phosphorescence.

"Climbed it before?" Ralph whispered. Olaf hated him for asking in front of the other boys.

The wind was rising from the ocean and twisting past the surge tank's slick surface, making the metal ring out. As long as Olaf could remember, the tower had been here, cleaving the landscape.

He knew what it was for: when the men needed to repair a turbine at the powerhouse, they had to turn off the river, funnelling all the dammed water down the mountain through the pen stalk and into the tank to let gravity absorb the surge. Now the tank was empty. A great blank dividing the sky. There was the dirty white of clam shells, the flashing tips of waves. And then there was this surge tank. Even in the rain it looked clean. Olaf and Greta had walked up to its base and touched it to see if the metal was warm or cold, but they never tried the ladder. It ran from the height of the tank and then stopped eight feet from the ground.

"To the very top?" Olaf asked Ralph.

"You climb the tank first, you get to drop out of school," Ralph said.

"You can't look down," Igmar yelled. "That's what kills you."

The boys all jumped onto a line of rain-wet logs and walked along them, silent again, hands in their pockets to prove they didn't need arms to balance. The rotting wood had softened and it crumbled under their steps. They reached the tank. They crouched together to pull a small log under the ladder, then dragged another to perch on top. The second log seesawed up and down. Knut held it still while the others climbed on top. One by one they balanced on the log—leaning back and forth—gripped the ladder and pulled themselves up, scurrying fast so the next boy could join them.

Ralph stood back, picking up rocks. Olaf nodded toward the tank. Ralph tossed a rock at it, a high ping. The boys above them stopped, looked down, then started again. Olaf and Ralph eyed each other awkwardly, Olaf tearing at a fingernail with his teeth, Ralph sliding his tongue along the cracks in his bottom lip. Knut waited, keeping the log steady.

Olaf cupped his hands together to form a holster for Ralph's foot. Ralph scattered the rest of his rocks across the sand, looked up again at the tank, then walked over to prop his foot in Olaf's palm. With a grunt Ralph hoisted himself up onto the log and leaned over to grip the ladder. He started to climb.

Salt air pushed open Olaf's lungs. His fingers were raw. He wanted to cheer something out to his friend. Ralph climbed a few more rungs, then Olaf reached for the ladder. He scrambled until he had his feet on it, and then he peered down at Knut who would have to climb up with no one underneath to help.

He'd been up ladders before. The first forty feet were easy. He felt a burst of energy as his boots pattered from rung to rung with a hollow clang, the ground receding beneath him. Olaf knew his father could walk up this thing easier than walking into his own kitchen.

But halfway up, the surge tank flared like a goblet, the top wider than the bottom, the sides jutting out at a thirty-degree angle over the beach. Olaf had to climb not just up, but out. With his arms stretched above him, his back hung parallel to the dark sea that crashed on the shore a hundred feet below.

The weight of his body pulled at his hands. He glanced down at the water. The view swayed too fast, lurching forward then retreating as his stomach turned. He clenched his eyes shut. His left foot slipped from the ladder and flailed. This leg suddenly felt longer than the other, heavier, the muscle pulling as the foot dangled in the air. He swung forward to hook the wayward heel over the rung, found his footing, pressed his face against the ladder's cold metal edge. He breathed. He could hear Knut breathing below. The rung of the ladder felt good under his boots.

If Greta were with him, she'd want to go down.

Someone up above was laughing. At first Olaf thought one of the boys was laughing at him. Ralph had almost reached the section of the ladder where it became perpendicular again. But he was clinging to the ladder without moving. It was Ralph who was laughing, only it didn't sound like Ralph; the laugh was high-pitched and fast, and it echoed off the surge tank's metal walls.

There was something wrong with Ralph. The laugh got sharper and sharper. Ralph screeched like a crow. Olaf's arms started to shake as if he were the one laughing. A ripple of air moved through his chest.

He wouldn't laugh. He was not going to laugh.

Ralph's arms were going to loosen. Laughter would slacken his muscles.

"Keep going," Knut shouted from below.

"I can't. It's not me," Olaf said. "Ralph has stopped. It's not me."

When Olaf looked up he saw that Ralph had swung to the side of the ladder to let him pass. Ralph was still laughing, but more quietly now. His feet were jammed tight together and he was hanging on with one arm. His body swayed out like a cupboard door.

Olaf clawed his fingers around the ladder's rungs, one hand over the next until he was sharing a rung with Ralph. He could keep only one boot on the ladder, tucking the other as close to the rung as he could. His left hand began to spasm. He could see the bottom of Igmar's, Joel's and Karl's boots moving higher then vanishing as the ladder straightened. A few more feet and Olaf and Ralph would reach the section where the ladder ran vertical. The ascent would be easier from there. Olaf opened his mouth to explain this, but something about Ralph's laugh made him stop. He wanted to climb away from it.

"Wait here," Olaf said. "Wait and we'll get you on the way down."

He climbed ahead. Looking down, he saw that Ralph was gripping the ladder again with both hands. Olaf felt lighter. The laugh coming out of Ralph faded. He knew he'd make it to the top.

Olaf was stepping into the sky. Beside him a seagull rolled on the air.

He curved around the tank where the ladder straightened again, his arms stretching ahead to find the rungs. When he got his grip, he had to let both feet hang out free before he could swing them back onto the ladder as he pulled himself up, his sweating palms squeaking on the metal. He climbed another eighty feet. The half-moon lit the edges of the surrounding clouds. A cobweb caught his cheek.

In the last stretch of the climb, the ladder narrowed, the rungs not rounded but flat. Their edges dug into his palms. Bits of rust stuck to his hands, flaked into his eyes. He tried to keep climbing with his eyelids clamped shut, but the surge tank started to tip.

The ladder seemed too narrow for a man. Olaf wondered who climbed up here and why he did it. A seagull swooped and cawed. Olaf waved at the too-close flap of its wings.

Above him the other boys had reached the top. Knut was a few rungs behind. Olaf couldn't hear Ralph at all.

He grabbed the last rung, swung himself up and folded his body over the edge of the roof, his arms dipping into shallow stagnant water.

The other boys watched him, Joel's face as white as the tank.

Three hundred feet. Olaf stood up.

The roof of the surge tank was as flat and white as the sides and the boys scattered like five peas on a plate. Rain had pooled on the surface. The boys all kicked at it—small explosions of water. They whacked their boots into the metal to hear it clang.

The wind answered. It sounded different than it did on the ladder, low and hollow, it didn't thud against the roof but whipped and whined across the surface as if trying to slide the boys right off.

Olaf leaned into this wall that pushed at his chest. His jacket was fat with air.

There were dead birds. A seagull, dark grey and rotting, its wings splayed out in a puddle. The feathers shimmied slightly as wind raked the water. And smaller birds, a blackbird, and what he thought were chickadees, although it was hard to tell in the dark. Their bodies were clumps. They reminded him of the mousetraps in the cookhouse, the cook walking to the woods with a dustpan full of eyeless tufts of fur. Did the birds fly here to die? Or was there something on the roof that killed them?

Olaf looked across the water at the lumps of islands, darker black than the black of the sky, each island rimmed in purple. He was higher than any tree. His father had never been this high.

Up the coast he could see the electric glow of the Powell River Mill—the light as yellow as the stink of sulphur. It lit the smoke that poured into the sky in four iridescent columns. Men were scurrying inside that box, masks over their faces as they released the spray of chemicals to turn trees into pulp. The lines of company houses were dim squares.

He turned to the south. If it were daytime, he'd be able to see all the way to Desolation Sound. A mile down the coast the moon caught the powerhouse's grey stone roof. All he could see was this roof, but he knew the front of the building had been painted to match the shore and trees, camouflage against enemy attack. The sides and back had been left as they were, the powerhouse greeting the ocean with this false face.

The Japs could attack now and Olaf could watch the planes swoop down and the incendiary bombs fall. The vibrations would rattle the surge tank and shake Ralph off the ladder. When his body landed on the beach it would snap like the sticks they held to play war.

Olaf looked up the coast at the sharp blades of the tree tops. He could reach over and pluck them from the ground.

Tug boats flickered green and red and white. In daylight the boats always looked happy, bobbing in the water, nudging log booms so much larger than themselves. He could not see the boom now, but knew it was there by the way it interrupted the water's ribbon of moon.

The Japs wouldn't bomb the ocean; they'd bomb the mill. The camps. He turned around and Tin Hat Mountain stretched out behind him. The mountain was a black mass, something inked out.

The logging camp where he lived was tucked behind the hill where the mountain dipped before it climbed again. He imagined his mother and sister in the wooden house. They were sitting by the stove and talking about where Olaf had gone. Across the table they passed his name back and forth. What I'm going to do to that boy, his mother said. She couldn't see him, way up here. Greta couldn't watch his hands. He stretched them up in the air.

"What's that ball for?" Joel asked him, pointing at a metal ball the size of a crouching man. It lay on top of the tank like a giant's toy.

"Lightning," Olaf said right away, and the boys nodded. His words lifted in the dark wind. "It captures lightning. It protects the surge tank." Olaf wasn't sure if this was really what it did, but the boys looked convinced. He could say anything up here and it would become true.

Olaf was the last to leave the roof. The others were kicking the birds off the tank, waiting to hear the splat and not hearing the splat so shoving at each other and asking who was scared, who was scared now, until one of them finally marched toward the ladder.

Olaf watched each head disappear.

When he grabbed it, the ladder was shaking. The wind and all that space down to the ocean dragged him forward, the urge to fall. He backed away from the ladder. Sure that the others couldn't see him, he got on his hands and knees and crawled. He turned to nudge his foot down until he could feel the third rung. He held on.

The flat edges dug into his palm. The wind pulled at his clothes. If he let go now, he would float.

It was harder going down, his arms and legs awkward with each backward step. His hands were growing numb. He counted as he descended. The seagulls had gone. What time was it now? He kept his eyes on his hands, dizzy with the effort not to look below.

The rungs of the ladder thickened. He reached the bend where it began to run diagonal. He had to curl himself around the corner, boot searching for a rung. He hinged from the hips, kicking his feet forward so they could catch the ladder while he kept his right hand on the straight section above. With his left hand he grasped the lower part of the ladder. The rust made his grip slide. To continue down, he was going to have to let go of his upper hand. He released his fingers, each one still frozen around the shape of the rung. He reached below for the ladder. His hand opened and closed on air.

He was falling backward. Then his fingers smacked the metal and he clasped the rung tight. His whole body began to tremble. Upside down in the sky.

Ralph was still there. As Olaf climbed slowly toward him, swaying his feet forward with each step so he could catch the next rung, he could see Ralph's arms rigid against the ladder. The laughing had stopped. Olaf had swallowed a flake of rust and it tickled his throat.

He coughed. It sounded like a laugh.

Ralph hooked one arm over the rung and one arm under it and leaned closer in.

"Ralph Forrest," Olaf said. The name ricocheted off the surge tank.

The wind tugged at Ralph's hair and flapped his jacket open. Olaf wondered if he had seen the birds the boys kicked off. Ralph squeezed to one side of the ladder so Olaf could pass.

Olaf climbed down until the two boys perched on the same rung, boots cramped in a line. Ralph pressed his cheek against the ladder.

"Go on," Olaf said. Below them there was the steady hollow clang of boots hitting metal. The other boys had climbed past Ralph. Were they going for help? The wind whistled through the ladder and whipped Ralph's hair across his eyes.

"Go on."

Ralph didn't move. The boys were nearing the bottom. Olaf dropped one foot to the next rung.

He waited. Ralph glanced down, snot running into his mouth. He wouldn't let go of the ladder long enough to wipe it away. His sleeve slipped to the elbow to reveal his arm taut with muscle and veins.

Olaf could still reach out and rest his palm on the nape of Ralph's neck to coax him down, but he didn't want to touch Ralph.

"Say something. Ralph. Talk. It will make it better." Bits of his words were torn by the wind.

Olaf waited.

Even the jaunty under-the-breath comments Ralph always made, even those he'd take.

Come on.

Go on.

Ralph was not going to move.

Olaf took another step down. He felt Ralph watch him. Three more steps, four, and he looked up through the black shapes of Ralph's boots. If Ralph let go without leaping free of the tank, his body would crash straight down and tear Olaf from the ladder and they both would drop to the earth.

As he neared the bottom, he climbed more quickly, careful not to look down until he was close enough to jump. Three yards from the ground, he leapt free with a high-pitched yell. He cleared the logs, landed on the balls of his feet, then rolled into the familiar crunch of sand and shells. He lay there for a moment, feeling the moist sand flat between his shoulder blades. Above the clouds, the stars looked as if someone had thrown a handful of rocks across the sky.

Ralph was still on the surge tank, but smaller. He hadn't moved. If Olaf didn't know Ralph was there, he wouldn't realize the dark speck was a boy.

Olaf scurried to his feet, rubbed shells and pebbles off his knees.

"You coming?" Karl yelled as he ran toward the water. The other boys ran too, jumping up and down on beach logs. The salt air was sharp on Olaf's face. Down by the ocean, the boys began to shout.

"Dumplings and gravy! Right now a whole plateful of dumplings and gravy!"

"Roast beef!"

Olaf couldn't tell who was saying what. His stomach spasmed. It was long past dinner. Greta and his mother would be eating without him. Greta would ask if she could have his portion and his mother would blow cigarette smoke across the table, say she always knew her son would do something like this, then slide his plate to Greta.

"No, flapjacks. A foot-high stack of flapjacks!"

"And bacon!"

"And bacon! Hey Ralph! We're going to have bacon!"

"Pork and beans!" one of them bellowed over the noise of the waves.

That's what Olaf wanted. They could stay out here all night and sit around a bonfire like the men do in the summer, heat a can over the flames. Ralph would climb down, shoulder Olaf for a space, grab a spoon. They wouldn't say how long he'd been up there. They'd eat. Olaf would have liked his tin lunch box right now, its slim black handle. He'd unfold his mother's wax paper and pass her bread pudding to the boys.

"Salmonberry pie!" Olaf heard his voice toss the words out into the wind. He was suddenly giddy. "Salmonberry pie!" He yelled up to Ralph as if he had a piece to offer. He could do this. He could just shout out what he wanted to eat.

Olaf turned to see where the boys were. They'd almost reached the trail that led to the road. If he didn't go now, he'd lose them.

"Salmonberry pie!" he shouted at the surge tank before breaking into a run.

When they reached the road, the other boys climbed onto the pile of bikes to rip out their own. Olaf was still running through the trail, but he could see the flicker of wheels through the trees. He caught up. They saluted Olaf and he saluted them back. He grabbed his bike. Ralph's bike was lying by itself. The tire was close to the road and Olaf thought maybe they should push it toward the trail.

The other boys wheeled off. The wind died down. His bike felt cold and wet. Without Greta to slow him, he'd be home in no time.

He pedalled back up the logging road. He flew into the camp and lifted his hands off the handlebars. The bike pitched to the left and he swayed his weight to the right and kept pedalling without holding on. The cookhouse was dark; the bunkhouses were dark; the men weren't sitting outside smoking or spitting tar. No one could see him now.

He careened along the trail to his home. Without taking off his boots, he walked through the back door and across the linoleum, pleased with the mud tracks, the wet slap of his soles on the floor.

The kitchen was empty.

The air smelled of stale smoke. He checked the stove. The pots were full of food that hadn't been served.

Balls of wool sat on the chesterfield, pierced by knitting needles, and he wished now for their comforting click, clack, his mother's sighs as she worked.

He leaned against the airtight heater to feel its warmth. Someone must be home. It was dangerous to leave a roaring fire when no one was home.

He stopped to listen. Rustle of fire in the airtight. Click of the pane against the sill. The wind had started blowing again, but more gently. He could hear his own breath, his blood pounding in his ears, the flick of his fingernail tearing at the skin of his cuticles. His steps were too loud as he walked slowly toward the stairs, heel to toe, his arms stiff by his side as if he were trying to find his balance.

A house has a face—from outside, but even from inside he could tell that the two windows above the sink were blank as untelling eyes. When he was a small boy, he used to be afraid of the house— not the creak of the stairs or the wind in the attic or even his bedroom closet where someone, something, could hide—he was afraid of the windows themselves, the glass that held the glowing light from the lamp, and these wooden walls that were as thick as a man's shoulders are broad. He thought the house could watch him, when he did something wrong, that it knew things that even his mother did not.

But the stairs tonight were reassuring to climb, each step wide

enough for his boots, his hand holding this familiar cedar banister that his father had sanded smooth and round as a candle. He
wondered if Ralph was still gripping the ladder's slick rungs. When
he reached the top of the stairs, he kept hold of the banister and
clenched his eyes shut as if this would stop Ralph from letting go.

Now he wanted to make a noise, cough or call out, anything to fill
the house. He thumped his hand on the doorframe as he marched
into his parents' room—dark. Into Greta's room, rapping first on the
open door although she wouldn't be able to hear. Moonlight caught
a book splayed on the floor, a page lifting on its own. Beside the
book was one of the Red Ryder comics Greta liked to sneak from
Olaf.

He sat on the unmade bed. He would give Greta the comic book,
to keep, when she came home. The promise tightened its grip on his
thoughts the way tangled sheets bind sleep.

He could give one comic to Greta and one to Ralph. No—more
than one. He would let them have as many as they wanted. Handing over his prized collection filled him with a sharp pleasing sense
of loss.

The wind rattled the glass against the frame. Underneath him were
Greta's heavy woolen blankets, he could lie down, fall asleep, feel the
rush of relief he always felt on waking up from a bad dream.

Outside, in the distance, his mother was calling him.

He pressed his boots firmly into the floor to hold her voice in
place.

She called again. He scurried downstairs and out the front entrance. The air was colder now that he'd been inside. He left the door
open and light spilled a jagged yellow triangle over the steps.

He ran through the trail. Up ahead, there was a thin white shimmer between the trees. His mother was standing alone outside in
her nightgown, the bulk of her overcoat hanging awkwardly over
it. When she saw Olaf, she ran toward him, almost tripping as she
opened her arms.

"Greta!" she called out, "Greta!" He wanted to shrink into his
sister's name.

His mother held him and he buried his face into the slick softness of the nightgown. "Greta—where is she? Is she back at the house? Olaf? Is she with you? Olaf? Where is your sister?" His eyelashes flickered against her warm chest. As long as he didn't answer her questions, he could keep his arms around her. "Greta?" she asked again. Her body stiffened.

"Mom, I didn't…"

"What did you do?"

"Mom, she…"

She pushed past him to run up the trail. He watched the back of her overcoat.

"She ran away," he yelled.

His mother stopped. She turned to face him. Her coat swung open and again he could see the white flicker of her nightgown.

"Greta raced down the road on her bike, before I knew where she was going, before I could catch her, she wouldn't do what I said, she wouldn't look, she wouldn't stop, she went speeding on her bike down the logging road, I couldn't see where she went."

"Greta…Greta did?" She walked back, her feet careful over stones and broken branches.

"I've…I've been looking for her. I didn't come home. I've been looking for Greta for hours." The lie stretched out to his mother and pulled her toward him.

"Where did you look?" she asked. Her voice was softer now. "The men have split up. They're all searching. Did you see your father?"

"The beach," he blurted out. He felt as light as he did on top of the surge tank. He could say anything. "I looked for her at the beach."

His mother nodded. She gazed out past his head. She pressed her hands together like she was praying, but she wasn't praying. Olaf took her arm, the bone under her nightgown under her coat, and led her back to the house.

Not until he shuffled her to the table—slipped off her coat, pulled out the cups for tea, put the kettle on the stove, slid her tobacco in front of her so she could roll a cigarette—did he realize that he knew where his sister had gone.

He walked outside and grabbed his bike, turned to see his mother standing in the light of the doorway. She looked afraid, the lamp-light shining through her gown and silhouetting her legs.

"Olaf," she cried. He liked her saying his name. He started to pedal down the path and she called it once more.

He careened down the logging road, then onto the main road that led to the surge tank, keeping his eyes on the spin of his front wheel. The ladder was on the other side of the tank, facing the ocean, so he couldn't see Ralph even if he looked.

The men were combing the shore. Olaf strained to track their voices. The loggers called out for his sister, then for him. His father led each call then the other voices joined in. The shouts trailed off and all the men stood silent as they waited for a response. Their bodies were still, black as paper cut-outs against the ocean's tumble. The woods absorbed the echo. Then the men began calling again, sway of lanterns etching the trees. Olaf imagined running down to show them he was safe—he'd throw his arms wide and announce where Greta had gone, spill the news like light. His father's face would lift, smile, he'd nod as if Olaf had made her appear.

He jumped off and pushed his bike to where the woods thinned. The men were small, visible only between the dark columns of firs. In the mist rising from the ocean, their lanterns bobbed like small floating moons.

They were nearing the surge tank. Light swung up against its surface. Someone had begun to carry a lantern up the ladder. Olaf dropped his bike and pushed his way past the trees, arching his head back to see the tower swooping into the sky so that the swirl of dark clouds seemed to be underneath his body instead of high above it—the sky was the ocean, the surge tank rocking in the waves. He had to grip a branch to steady himself.

Ralph was still holding on.

Olaf grinned and wrapped his arms around his chest, rubbing his hands up and down to get the blood moving. He thought of Ralph's hair lifting in the wind.

With a shiver he realized that the climbing man was his own father, the familiar wide shoulders rising quickly up and up and it was strange now to see his father chart the same height that Olaf himself had climbed, his father's body so high and yet shrunken against the expanse of white—a man crouching down to join a boy's game. His father's steps were too heavy, his boots would shake the rungs and make the remaining birds fall from the top of the tank, wingless carcasses dropping the length of the tower like secrets, each one landing in a waterlogged splat.

The birds were dead already. Olaf was not responsible for the birds.

Ralph had managed to climb down to where the tank ran vertical again but now he had stopped. He was waiting for Olaf's father.

Olaf had seen his father climb this high many times before. His father could reach this high or higher each time he rigged a new spar tree, climbing it and then topping it and wrapping the guyline confidently around the tree's tip as tight as a noose. He could climb the spar while waving down at Olaf, then reach the top and smoke a cigarette and take off his hat and pass it through the air as if collecting rain and even as he sat on the flat top of the tree without his belt roping him to it, even as he perched with nothing to hold him to the trunk's quivering height running straight down to the ground that lay so solid under Olaf's feet, his father was tipping his hat to him and so his father was attached to him and would not fall.

Now his father was hatless, hand over hand to reach another man's son. He did not turn to wave.

When his father reached Ralph, he plucked the boy's fingers from their tight grip on the rungs and wrapped the boy's arms around his shoulders. From the ground Olaf could no longer see Ralph. His black shape had disappeared inside the man's so that they moved as a single body.

Olaf got back on his bike, pedalling fast through the trees that swayed toward his face until he feared he'd lose his balance. The sound of the wheels mimicked the crying sounds he imagined Ralph would make. The men would wrap him in one of their Mack jackets. The men would offer him a sip of moonshine from one of the flasks they kept in their canvas satchels and then Olaf's father would lean down to speak to the boy at his own level, gazing into his eyes the way he looked into Olaf's whenever he wanted the truth.

There's a look a child gets when he has something good to tell, when he knows something valuable that an adult wants. At first Ralph would say nothing, letting the moonshine dilate the blood vessels in his fingers and his feet. Olaf knew that warm sensation. Olaf had come in from the cold to feel his frozen fingers softening and opening as soon as his father's whiskey was in him, as if his hands and not his mouth had drunk the amber brew. To sit like that with his father beside the airtight, warmth outside his skin and inside his skin—Olaf would have told him anything.

Now Olaf turned down another trail a mile north of the surge tank toward the cragged beach where the boats and houses sat unused. The woods swallowed him. Then the forest exploded with music, one high-pitched voice then something like a fiddle. His bike rattled over branches, in the dark he couldn't see the forest floor. With each bounce the music tried to shake him off. The trail opened onto the beach.

Every window of the Jap house was lit. The building was leaning slightly toward the ocean, close to the water like a beached boat, squares of light doubled by a rippled reflection.

The music was coming from inside, the volume cranked so high that the windowpanes were shaking, sound tinny and broken. The house's slanting walls seemed too fragile to hold it.

A lull in the music. He heard Greta, her low rocking voice. Her singing slid left and right of the tune. She flitted by the glass. The flames of oil lanterns followed her wake. He dropped his bike and crept to the house to watch her as she swooped back and forth across his view, a flash of blue that appeared, disappeared, dancing from one end of the kitchen to the other, her hair a swirl of light around her head as she leapt from a stool into the air.

He pressed his face to the glass and felt the vibrations of the music the way she would, the pulse vibrating his jaw.

She landed in a heap of blue satin. Lanterns flickering all around her, on the table, the counter, the floor. The robe covered her body like a tarp, spilled over her feet, shiny blue with red piping and red pictures stitched down the sides, small houses and smaller people and enormous curving fish. Greta grasped the satin, then she was up again, swooping around the kitchen in this robe that skimmed over the jerky quickness of her limbs. As she brushed past the table, a sleeve caught at a rice bowl and dragged it to the table's edge.

The bowl didn't fall. Greta swayed her head back and forth to the vibrations of the record, her mouth slack. No words in her singing.

It bothered Olaf, the sounds that meant nothing, her low voice flooding this house where she didn't belong. The family that had lived here had been lined up with the others, bussed out, without a chance to pack their things.

Greta reached her arms up and spun in place. The robe twisted at her feet. Its long red tie whipped a lamp. The robe was going to catch on fire. He banged at the window. The latch was jammed shut.

She kept dancing. He ran around to the other side of the house to reach the door.

The night air rushed in as he entered the room. Greta stood still. She didn't jump or call out. She stood with her back to Olaf. He couldn't see her expression, couldn't tell if she knew it was him. The record kept turning, the robe corkscrewed around Greta's legs.

He walked toward her. He thumbed the lantern to the middle of the table, the bowl away from the edge. There was another bowl lying mouth-down on the counter, the shards of a plate on the floor. The cupboard doors were open. Across the table she had shaped the letter *B* from grains of rice.

"Greta, it's me." He tugged at the robe. She signed something to him, but the sleeves covered her hands. He felt her fingers flicker against the satin.

She spun from his grasp, climbed onto the counter and tore open a box of crackers, waving it in front of his face like some toy she had stolen and wouldn't give back.

You left me, her lips shaped the words as she stuffed crackers into her mouth. She swayed her head side to side.

I was there, Olaf signed.

Gone, she signed back.

I was there. It was you. You didn't see me. But his hands were small and tight: even his fingers didn't believe him. The music stopped— vinyl crackle and static. The kitchen was white with silence. Then the roar of water as the ocean hit the shore.

She said something, but she kept eating and the crackers muffled the shape of her words. His stomach clenched at the sight of food, but he wouldn't take a thing left behind by the family. Through the bedroom door, he could see another lantern, records strewn across the bed. He slipped a bowl from the counter and put it back on the table, slid the other bowl to meet it, the clink of china ringing out as the two rims touched.

Gone gone gone, she signed, shimmied down from the cupboard and traipsed around the kitchen with her hands forming the words wider and wider. But she wasn't upset. She was grinning now. Olaf would like her to be upset. He would like her to sit down.

We could stay gone all night. We could sleep here.

"We have to go home." His voice cracked. "Mom is waiting for us."

Gone gone gone. She spun around as she signed.

She swooped by Olaf again and he grabbed her by the waist, expecting her to squirm against his grip. Like a dead weight she collapsed into his chest. He held this feeling, her leaning against him, him bracing her, him keeping her from falling, if he stepped away she'd slump to the floor. "I'm here," he whispered. He mouthed the words against her cheek. She was breathing fast from the dancing, but she let him hold her, the way one of the camp whiskey jacks will step forward to peck at a palm full of seeds offered by an owner who has been gone too long. Through the slick satin Olaf was relieved to feel the rough nubs of her sweater underneath.

When he released Greta, the warmth of her body fell away from his. She stepped free of the robe, letting it drop to the floor. He bent down to pick it up, walking into the other room to place it on the bed, folded on top of the records. Two of the records were chipped, another had been cracked. He hoped it wasn't Greta who did it. He couldn't tell which broken parts were new.

She watched him shut each cupboard door in the kitchen, the flat warm sound of wood on wood. One by one he blew out the lanterns. The rooms shrunk. Greta took his hand and swung it as they walked out the door. This bothered him too, the music in her arms, and when they reached his bike, he turned to check the house. The windows were dark. He let Greta sit on his seat and he stood up to pedal. When they had almost reached the logging road he began to get tired and he remembered that she must have ridden her own bike to the Jap house but it was too late now to go back. Her hands gripped his waist and the bike rocked with the effort of his legs as he followed the narrow track his wheels had left.

LALITA AND THE BANYAN TREE

SHUBHA VENUGOPAL

Lalita never planned to fall in love with a tree. The women noticed first. They could not fail to observe Lalita's skin-glow. She looked like she had swallowed one of her *diyas*—tiny brass candlehold-ers with *ghee*-soaked wicks—and the flame illuminated her from within. The women's faces, however, drooped like sunflowers aban-doned by sun as Lalita's had also once done. And so they watched and wondered at the tree.

When Lalita finally merged with the tree she wore the guise of mourning. Her widow's hair flowed like Ganga River, free of knots or braids. No bloodred *bindi* dotted her forehead—smooth as fresh-ly-churned cream. No *mangalsutra* bound her throat; no bangles en-circled wrists. Her *sari*, never exposed to the stains of dyes, gleamed white and pure in the sun. Barely eighteen, she flapped near its branches like a broken dove. Touched, the tree realigned her wings.

Lalita became betrothed to a local man at the late age of thirteen though most girls married at five. In this remote village in India's hills, ancient rules reigned and women accepted, resigned. Lalita's father, angry at having no sons, decided to utilize his only daughter. She would serve him, he declared, until she turned thirteen. "But who will want her then?" her mother wailed to the monkeys that chattered on the riverbank.

Several monkeys stopped their babble, scratched behind their ears, and pulled ticks from their hides. Not knowing the answer, they continued to speak in tongues. Lalita, then aged six, saw her mother's hands bleed as she wrung out clothes in the river and beat them dry against a flat rock with only a monkey-chorus and a daughter to watch.

For as long as she could remember, Lalita crawled and ducked away from her father's hand. Once, when she was four, she stood rigid as a stone temple pillar between her father and mother. She did not want his *chappal* to slap her mother's cheek, leaving behind slipper-prints. Her mother made herself a shadow in the corner. She called to Lalita, telling her to run, to not worry. Her father's foot drew back. Lalita spit on his toes. He glinted like a snake and moved to strike.

With him behind her, Lalita flew through a nearby field swarming with yellow butterflies. Temple bells tolled in the distance. Distracted, unable to see, her father tripped into smears of cow dung as butterflies danced before his eyes. From then on only stealth gained him the prize of kicking his daughter's thighs.

Lalita learned to keep silent and to hide in the forests. She learned to listen to the cautioning of monkeys' cries and the darting of lizards' forked tongues. She knew her father was near when the deer flattened their ears and raised limbs, nostrils quivering as they readied for flight. She sniffed for his scent lifted in the breeze and masked her fleeing footsteps behind rumbles of river over rocks. By heeding nature's signs she was able to escape his grip.

But soon another man whom she could not so deftly defy possessed her. When she turned thirteen her father, afraid to disobey divine dictates, fulfilled the *kanyaadan*—men's sacred duty to marry off daughters. But the village men declared her too old, said they wanted more tender child-brides. Monthly blood, flowing like tides pulled by the moon, already polluted her; she was no longer desired. Only an aged ox-cart driver remained to claim his bride. Squinting and almost blind, body bent and exposing an egg-sized lump on the back of his neck, he sidled up to her and, after sizing her up, he pinched her upper arm. Licking his lips, he fingered the berry-ripe spot left behind. He agreed to take her off her father's hands with a dowry of their best milk-rich cow.

Quick with the whip that he lashed across the heads and backs of beasts, he rode Lalita as he rode his ox. Each night before straddling her body with his head thrown back, he placed his whip on a table near her sight. She felt sometimes it would come alive and coil itself around her neck. In those times she barely let herself breathe.

Lalita, swift enough to avoid his whip during the day, could not evade him at night. She could not roll free from the weight of his thighs gripping and bruising her sides. She could not stay dry when his sweat dripped onto her belly and breasts, or prevent his unwashed, mud-and-animal scent. She learned her only defense.

Ignoring her husband's grunts, her body unresisting as earth, she imagined herself bathed in ripples of moon swaying to the music of God Krishna's flute. Peacocks shimmered and preened in these dreams. A lotus, pink and tantalized, slowly opened in a pond. Jasmine-scented air grew damp with her longing. In her mind she laughed with mockingbirds and sang with *maina* birds, *koyals* and larks.

For five years she lived as a village man's wife. Silent, she bore the weight of water on her head as she carried earthen pots from the river to her abode. She grew thirsty from heat, but could not take time to drink. Like other girls costumed as women, she bent her back and ruined her knees working hunched over in the rice, sugar cane, and vegetable fields. The skin on her hands cracked and bled. She gathered vegetables that she rid of insects, cut, sliced, and assembled, for her husband's daily meals.

She collected cow dung, soon immune to its smell. She spread it out to dry, and patted it gently with her hands into patties used for fuel. She wove straw and plastered it with mud to make thatched-roof huts, and she learned to wait until night to scrape with a sharp rock mud caked in her nails. She molded, teased, and caressed wet clay into kitchen pots. She touched the clay in the way she could never touch a person. Like the other girls, she dipped twisted cloths into boiled plant dyes until rainbows discolored her hands. She wrung and patted, shaped and molded, cleaned and washed and cooked and carried, and let him spread her legs, and slowly dissolved within her skin.

Until the day her husband died, leaving her free, and Lalita fell in love with a tree.

The women swear it happened on the day of the festival of lights. On that day, when prayers were chanted at dawn as orange rays ruptured clouds, when hundreds of *diyas* lit doorways and paths, windows and yards, when *patakas* crackled and burst and village girls whirled in flaring, celebration-skirts, Lalita blazed with a secret. At first they thought it might just be the reflected flicker of lamps that shone in her eyes. The festival lights could not compare to Lalita, sun-radiant and smiling as she left the town behind. The women plotted to figure out why. They could not know, of course, that the sparks were ignited weeks before, while her husband, condemned by a fever consuming him like rage, tossed and ranted on his deathbed.

Weeks before the day of the festival of lights, as her husband groaned in his sleep and as the world wept monsoon tears, Lalita wandered to the windowsill. As the *rakshasi* wind wailed her demon-loud howls, Lalita grew restless. Her feet could not stay still and insisted on beating in time with the rain. Her breath heaved along with the squalls. She nibbled on wet lips. Her arms, bearing the bruises of her husband's handprint, opened to embrace the blackening day. She went outside into the downpour. Her *sari* melted against her flesh like petals drenched upon darkened boughs. Her hair streamed into her eyes.

Drawn to the lurching, drunken river with waves frothing and foaming at the tips, she did not waver in her stride. Following the gush of the torrents, Lalita rushed along the river's side, letting it be her guide. She passed woodland and field—terrain as identifiable to her as the lines on her hands. Farther and farther she ran, past the village's edge. She ran until she no longer recognized the river's twists and turns, and the alien land. Her footsteps slowed to a halt then and she drew closer to the bank. Weary, she prepared to let the river-mud, like a reclaiming womb, pull and suck her in. She was waist-deep in water when she heard the calling of leaves disturbed. She knew, from the clarity with which she heard this call, that this was no mere dream.

Lalita half-swam, half-waded, past an unfamiliar river bend. Soon, out of the gloom, a banyan tree materialized. Its roots and branches overflowed the horizon. Within its network of limbs it captured and held patches of silvery sky. She thought of wrapping those sky-bits around her like a quilt. With its slender fingers and veined, muscular arms the tree summoned her. She responded. Dragging herself from the river she crawled to it through the clinging, needy soil. She reached out. It felt solid and real to her touch.

Panting and only half-alive she draped herself over a dry patch of earth under the banyan's aerial roots. Within its strange caverns with their damp, ventilated walls the wind grew tame. Calmed by melodies of echoing wind, she stopped weeping and let herself sleep. For two days she slept as her husband, at home, drew his last punishing breaths. For two days the tree bent over her like a lover and kept her cool and safe, free from deadly fevers. Her sighs became less tremulous. Her eyelids stopped fluttering; her lips now could be still. Night and day, day and night, she slept.

Some mornings later, a lush covering of dew left her damp with anticipation. She found herself cradled in fissures of sun-soaked earth between hanging roots, brown and tender as her own skin. Never had she felt so warm, so moist, like a ripening fruit. High in a shag of leaves, bats flapped in sleep and brilliant bee-eaters snacked with motionless bodies and a whirring of wings. Herons, blooming on branches like magnolias, swung their elegant necks. Mice scampered in delight. Monkeys flicked their tails, sinuous and nimble in the dawn. Hungry, Lalita stretched her limbs and reached for *beir*. She spit out the seeds and shuddered as the sweetness exploded on her tongue. She sipped from rain cupped in a curved leaf, quenching her thirst. The hum and the drone penetrated her silence, pulsing, intensifying, until she arched her back in response. Exhausted, satisfied, she felt her body loosen and go soft.

After hours of languishing in the shade and dozing in the sun, she meandered from inside the banyan tree and leaned over a nearby pool to wash her flushed face. The tree leaned over her shoulder. She saw her watery form ringed with its emerald leaves. She touched the sparkling waves of her face, surrounded by precious leaf-gems. She turned to the tree and, bold now, threw her body against its trunk. She rubbed her palms over its knots and bumps, its ancient lines that held within them the passing of time. She pressed her mouth into the bark and breathed, her sigh fragrant as *raatkirani*, the night-blooming flower queen. The tree shook. With its winding, powerful limbs it held her close.

Weeks later, when Lalita left the *divali* celebration, the village women followed her. Provoked by the clarity of Lalita's skin, by her forest eyes, they gathered one night after their men had burned Lalita's husband, whom a wandering village boy had found dead in his bed, on the funeral pyre. The women crept, silent as vines, along the banks of the river as Lalita glowed ahead— a white shimmer against black, enchanting in moonlight. With her *sari* blowing behind her, Lalita flew over jagged rocks and broken twigs, desire spurring her feet. The women stumbled, not used to running in the night. Their ankles swollen from bearing the weight of sons and their bodies bluish from years of work, they grumbled but continued on, past the village's edge and around the river's bends. Then they saw Lalita, encased in a banyan tree, her back pressed against bark. Mumbling amongst themselves, they returned to their homes. That night, as their husbands lumbered clumsy upon them, the women thought of Lalita—her head cradled by vegetation and feathers from birds, her body cushioned in soft, giving dirt.

The next week, as their husbands snoozed in the heat of midday and children busied in play, the women sneaked out to watch Lalita and the banyan tree. They saw her clearing rotting debris out from one of the tree-rooms, cool and green beneath aerial roots. Her hips swung and rocked to a song. The women leaned closer to hear. They never knew she could sing. Her tune followed them home. Later, as they worked in the sugar cane fields, they practiced indulging. Their husbands complained; their children yelled. Their throats quickly went hoarse.

By the next time they went, Lalita's body had healed. Her *sari* lay out to dry upon a rock and she wore only her blouse and petticoat. No hints of her beatings remained. She sat, a golden bronze-like statue, on a branch, and rubbed oils collected from plants and herbs into her hair and skin. She glistened, slick as leaves after rain. Light reflecting off the bougainvilleas tucked above her ears created dappled patterns upon her black hair. The women looked at one another, at their split, bleeding lips, at their straw-brittle skin. Wrinkles changed their faces, sorrows dark like berries marred their eyes. Their cheeks sagged into hollows. Stretch marks tracked their bellies and crisscrossed over breasts. Like the banyan's figs, their bruised flesh slipped into purple. Their disappointment hung from them like the bats on the banyan's boughs. That evening as they bathed their children in the river, they caressed their babies' fresh flesh and they dreamed of Lalita.

On the next trip they witnessed a change in the tree, for Lalita had fully moved in. In her quiet, whispering room she had made herself a little home. A dugout space in the ground served as her oven. By its side she had lined fruits and vegetables collected from woods and fields. Crushed herbs neatly sorted on piles of leaves separated by twigs gave her spice; sugar cane sweetened her meals. She drank milk from her dowry cow that she had brought along and that nestled in an adjacent tree-space. Freed from its lashings, the ecstatic cow gifted Lalita its thickest, frothiest milk. The tree expanded with the joy of Lalita's scents, her laugh, her movements. The women went home to meals they cooked for indifferent husbands and unruly children with only the worst parts left over for them.

They began to imagine how the banyan felt when touched by Lalita; how Lalita felt when touched by the banyan. Compared to the tree's might their husbands looked weak. Compared to its muscled trunks their husbands' limbs sagged. Compared to the color of its bark their husbands appeared pallid as decaying river fish. Compared to the lushness of its crown their husbands' scalps seemed dry and bald as waterless riverbeds. Compared to the sweet sounds of its birds their husbands' words seemed embittered, and compared to the tree's fragrance their husbands emitted breath stale as air entombed in caves. They went back and forth from the tree to their village until one day, the women decided to quit. Ignored by their husbands, left alone to face the elements, like Lalita, they chose the tree.

One month after the festival of lights, by the glow of dawn, the women snaked over the now-familiar terrain toward Lalita and the banyan tree, leaving their sleeping men. They went bearing infants on their hips, toddlers in tow. They found her rinsing her hair in rainwater. They approached and surrounded her—mothers turned into lost, bleating lambs. She smiled and invited them inside. From dawn until dark, with Lalita's help, the women settled in.

Among the banyan's spacious roots the women nestled and bloomed, each in her private room. As mothers rocked babies the tree rocked mothers. Some sang, some slept, some wept, some sucked on figs. They rested on mounds of soil, their arms and legs entwined with tree limbs. They bathed naked in the river, with sun dotting their skin. They feasted on jackfruit and mangoes gathered from the woods and let the juice dribble unchecked down their chins. They leaned their breasts upon low branches and let the tree take the weight from them. Like Lord Krishna with his beloved *gopis*, the tree multiplied.

Late that morning, the men of the village awoke confused and rubbed fingers caked with fertilizer into their eyes. The sting blinded them. No food waited ready to warm them; no wives knelt by their sides. They paced and called, they cursed and swore, to no avail. An empty pot rolled along the village path, trapping the echoing wind. For nearly two hours they hunted in vain for their wives. Tired from tilling the land, sore from sowing the seeds, they ached for their women, for their healing hands to knead away pain. Reality beset them. With whom would they celebrate the harvest? Who would help them gather the wheat? Who would help store it, bind it and prepare it for sale? With whom would they pray to the Gods of sun and rain? How could a village stay alive without any wives? The men, who trumpeted like elephants when they called out their wares in the village fairs, had no voices to acknowledge loss.

And then one of the men remembered a young woman with the sheen of morning upon her skin, with the clothes of mourning draped over her supple silhouette. He shared his memory and the men grew excited, recalling how their wives had whispered a name that rustled through their homes like wheat in gusts of wind. Lalita. The young woman once used like an ox by a husband more brute than man. The men had not liked her husband, had not liked the intensity of his abuse, but they had never thought to interfere. A man could do as he liked, after all, with his own wife. But what had happened to Lalita after the death of that man? Was that what their wives had gone to find out?

The men went to Lalita's house on the village outskirts, and finding it bare, continued their search, hoping to spot their wives. They followed the river as it wound ahead; they stopped often to look around.

One man, who lived near the edge of the village, peered out of his sagging doorway upon hearing the commotion. Lalita's father, feeble now with curved back and walking cane, hadn't heard such noise in a year. Since the death of Lalita's mother—a death by drowning in the river that he termed an accident—his body and house had fallen into disrepair. Rain flowed through his roof, soaked the floor, and made his bed feel perpetually damp. The mice he failed to catch and kill left droppings in his path. Two birds, defiant, built a nest near a hole in the roof and roused him to cursing with chirping each dawn and dusk. He barely ate, living on leftover rice, vegetable peels and overripe fruit left out behind villagers' homes that he pilfered as they slept. Without a wife to slap or a daughter to kick, his muscles hung weak and unused from his aging frame.

When he heard the men—men from the village who had forgotten him—he came out and struggled to track them as they raced ahead on their quest.

The men's quest led them out of the village's realm and into a different land. For the first time they observed the landscape—the wild formations of silver-gray rock jutting from patches of dirt, the depth and greenness of forest and fields, the sudden stillness of birds, and the deer watching with one leg delicate and raised. In seeking clues to their missing wives, the men, and behind them, Lalita's father, discovered the world around them. They trailed the river until they passed a bend.

Then the men halted and witnessed their wives. Their wives' lotus-shaped eyes opened, drinking in the sun. Their midnight hair streamed. Their smooth sandalwood skin, their sinuous limbs: the men had never seen such a sight.

When he arrived, Lalita's father saw Lalita high up on a branch.

Towering above all of them stood a banyan tree that had multiplied its trunks, its free-hanging roots, its multitude of emerald leaves.

The men looked up and to each side, stunned by the size of the tree and by the way its roots cradled the women. The generosity of the tree, which could both contain and fulfill, made them feel small. And so they shrank themselves. With knees bent and arms crossed over legs, they squatted not far from the base of its roots and prepared to watch.

They watched as women held hands and leaned their heads close. Had they ever looked so into their wives' eyes? The men admitted not. They watched as one woman, with healing tree leaves, wiped at salt streaks on another's cheek. Had their wives cried? The men never thought to ask. They watched as one wife rubbed her bare arm against a smooth branch; back and forth, back and forth she massaged, until they, hypnotized, wished she would rub so against them. Had they touched their wives like that? Had their wives ever *really* touched them? The men wondered why not. They watched as women, with bodies yielding and pliable as moss, hung over the tree's handsome limbs. Had they ever let their women so loosen themselves? The men remembered their own voices sharp with endless demands.

Hungry from the lack of home cooked meals, and lonesome in homes where their words bounced off walls, returning to them, the men decided to get their wives back.

"But what must we do?" asked each man to the other, stumbling over the never-before spoken requests. Not finding an answer, not able to approach their transfigured wives, they had no choice but to wait instead. And so they listened, sitting quiet and still, until finally hearing the tree's gentle reply. While Lalita sang from her lofty perch, the tree joined her in verse, and in so doing, responded to the men's request.

It was then that the men heard the sounds of the tree: its calming wind tunes, the tapping of twigs, the beating of wings, the humming of life. Before they had heard only the noises emitted by themselves—the rustling of their clothes, the grumbling in their throats, their own voices and breaths, their own blood rushing in circles within their own heads. The men discovered now how to perceive a world outside of them. They remained rooted to the ground. Except for Lalita's father.

After listening to the duet of daughter and tree, Lalita's father stepped forth from the tree's long network of shadows and moved past the dowry cow trembling nearby. He dropped his cane, stood up straight, and walked over roots with feet lifted high. He glanced up at Lalita and turned away, embarrassed at how little he had known, at how much she had grown. When he reached the branches beneath her, he pulled himself up, scratching his legs and bruising his arms, until he sat panting on a thin limb not far from his daughter. He rubbed his cheek against the tree's bark and felt its answering vibrations. Wet streaks from his withered cheek stained the banyan's bark.

Lalita's father lifted his face and looked fully at his radiant daughter. Startled at his bold look, Lalita drew away. But, on seeing the awe in his eyes, she relaxed and stretched out her hand. With a moan that startled birds and scattered mice, he bowed his head and touched the hem of his daughter's white *sari* that fluttered above his eyes.

"*Hai Bhagavan!*" he murmured, then shouted, as he thanked God for the sight of this daughter, transformed into a goddess by a deity-tree that held her like a consort.

Lalita joined in his *bhajan*, his worship-song, her pitch matching his. When they first saw Lalita's father, the women didn't speak, but now they joined in the *bhajan*. The men, who had shaken their heads and prepared to spit at the sight of an old man climbing towards his once-beaten daughter, also sang. Soon the air rang with their chants.

When the men's lungs ached with song and their mouths felt too dry to continue, they went to their wives with open arms. They bent their heads to the tree's roots, as they would do to the feet of a god. Only a god could humble them.

Like a temple, the tree gave them shelter. Drops fallen from leaves purified the men like holy water. Fruits growing near the tree became their *prasad*. The wives, who saw their men's actions, delighted in such devotion. Banyan-blessed and wife-caressed, the men felt soothed and calm.

Years later, after Lalita and her father began to converse while sitting in banyan branches, after the men understood how to listen to the wisdom of a tree, after they petted and wheedled their wives, begging them back to their homes, after the village rang with temple chimes, the legend of Lalita and the Banyan Tree continued to be recited like a prayer-chant. Lalita, who learned how to find herself, taught the people the way to look. The tree, which willingly spread itself, taught them how to expand. Roots freely sprang from mother trunks and turned into trees that then let out more roots. The banyan tree stretched across the world.

WITHOUT GOOD-BYES

MICHAEL WISNIEWSKI

Hoggin arrives here every NFL Sunday at pretty much exactly 11:30, after he goes to church and the A&P, then walks his way over. He needs to walk because he doesn't have a license because he isn't completely there. He doesn't *look* that off-kilter; you could drink beside him for an hour before you'd know he's not right. His mind has maybe a 10 per cent deficit: just enough that he'll never do better than his job as a greeter in the Wal-Mart. In fact, he lives across from the Wal-Mart, in a complex for people of his caliber, a former motel the state now subsidizes to cater to mostly men, but also a few women, who still barely earn their rent and groceries and hopefully think enough to use birth control.

When he gets here, he claims his stool up at the very middle of the bar, sets his plastic A&P bag eight inches to his right, then orders a salmon on toast and two roast beef sandwiches with extra pickles, and he always eats the taller of the roast beefs first, then the salmon, then the other roast beef. The two stools that flank him are usually empty, but not because we shun him—it's just that, among other things, he has a habit of talking to no one in particular, and it can drive you bonkers sitting next to him. Even if you've known what his deal is for years, he'll say something quietly, and you'll catch yourself thinking he's talking to you, but he isn't. He's just getting out his words. A few every hour or so, and he's fine.

Still, you can imagine why, when I'm in here, I don't mind seeing a new face or two. You know, shake the place up a little. And this being a sports bar, you now and then do get a new face. Some Mc-Mansion owner's large-screen is on the blink and he needs to catch a game, or some Wall Street honcho is up here fishing and he's had enough nature and wants to burn down a whiskey. These kinds of people. I like when they're here.

Of course there's always the proverbial exception. Take for example this wise guy bookie from Brooklyn who once waltzed in here with his girlfriend the stripper. I don't need to tell you how a situation like this can go awry, or maybe I do. Let's just say you don't go bringing a stripper into a sports bar and expect to watch an entire NFL game without anyone hitting on the stripper. For one, she's bored by the middle of the first quarter. And if she has implants, as this one did, she's going to have every regular's eye in the place, even Hoggin's, laid on her by half time; and by the fourth quarter you have a drunk enough population in the bar that, as soon as the wise guy strolls off to the can to relieve himself, someone *will* approach her.

In the case of this stripper, the guy who approached her was Dorsey.

Dorsey and I go way back. We went to college together, which was so long ago it usually feels like it never happened—even though, because of it, we have the kinds of jobs we have. I'm a mid level electrical engineer for Con Ed, and Dorsey is an attorney—not your high-powered kind, but he does scrape up his mortgage payments given the inevitable squabbles around town. Anyway, Dorsey's a Jets fan and the Jets are getting their asses handed to them, and Dorsey has his usual C-note on the game—he always takes the Jets against the spread, which proves admirable loyalty but also a definite level of stupidity—and as a result he's drinking more quickly than usual, and we Giants fans have been riding him since the Jets' third fumble, so, to get away from us, I imagine, he moseys over to the stripper while the wise guy from Brooklyn is off taking a piss, and engages her in conversation. Now Dorsey's not going to fuck her—he's married, like me, and our days of catting around behind our wives' backs are long since over—but he is drunk, and she does have those implants, which she made apparent just after entering the place by taking off her black leather jacket *and* pink cashmere cardigan, and she is a stripper, which some people might say doesn't mean jack, but my point is you don't take money from strange men to dance naked between their legs unless you're a little, how shall we say, *comfortable* with the opposite sex.

So there they are, the bored stripper proud of her implants and their effect on men, Dorsey hopeless about the Jets and vaguely distraught about what has become of his life since law school, and she's not exactly rebuffing him—in fact, he's making her laugh—and here comes the wise guy, back from the can. At first the wise guy just sits on his stool beside her, which, by the way, happens to be one of those normally vacant stools directly beside Hoggin, and he, the wise guy, pretends to watch the six televisions behind the bar, glancing from one to another to dash any question about whether he's a bookie with action on every game up there. I think to go over and yank Dorsey toward us regulars, but it occurs to me that he isn't doing anything wrong, just talking to make a human being laugh, and that it would be cruel to rush him back to the Jets' latest debacle and the truth that he's only hours from another Sunday night wherein he'll sober up and face the grind of another workweek—or keep drinking, only to arrive at his office the next morning hung over, which, rumor has it, means he'll make some legal-schmegal head fake that'll botch one of the few cases he's got going that involve more than a broken leg. And he's still trying to get the last of his kids through college, and pay off the loans his wife took out when *she* went to college to become a nurse, and she was just laid off because another hospital in Westchester closed, and the taxes on his house doubled last spring even though he used his professional expertise to fight them—so, with all this in mind, I keep my distance from him and the stripper, milking my longneck and hope in the three hundred I have on the Giants, who are scheduled to play the night game.

Then I see the wise guy turn and say something to Hoggin, and

Hoggin doesn't respond, just opens his A&P bag, then pulls out his usual half gallon of A&P vanilla bean ice cream, along with the large silver serving spoon he bought years ago from a tag sale and always brings from his place in the complex for people who aren't all there. Of course, this is pure innocence on Hoggin's part, just Hoggin doing what Hoggin always does every Sunday with exactly seven and a half minutes to go in the fourth quarter of the second NFL game, but the wise guy, of course, doesn't know this. From the wise guy's point of view, Hoggin has probably just mumbled something, very likely some obscure statistical insight he absorbed last week from a discarded *Daily News*, and the wise guy has tried to parlay this mumbling into an attempt at conversation that will: a) acquire another gambler for his bookmaking business, or at least b) make it appear as if he, the wise guy, doesn't care that the stripper might have the hots for Dorsey—but Hoggin has snubbed the wise guy in favor of the cheapest ice cream in the continental U.S. Worse, when Hoggin opens the half-gallon carton, which he does, as always, after making sure it's centered perfectly in front of him and exactly parallel to the edge of the bar, as well as after tucking a sky blue A & P napkin, also pulled from the bag, under the collar of his button-down shirt, the contents of the carton are, as always, soupy. This just happens to be the way Hoggin *must have* his ice cream, which, by the way, is his purposefully delayed dessert after the salmon and roast beef sandwiches he finished before the first game's opening kickoff, and his ritual in enjoying it as such is no doubt his way of forestalling yet another week of his own grind— as a greeter at the Wall-Mart—but the wise guy is new to all this. From the wise guy's point of view, this Sunday of watching football in a quaint sports bar in Putnam County instead of some crammed hole in Brooklyn has now entered a phase he can't comprehend or tolerate: He is, just like that, losing control of a life that was fine until he had to push things by treating his stripper girlfriend to a weekend upstate to see orange and red leaves.

Even worse, once Hoggin starts in on that melted ice cream, he doesn't stop. He is going to eat all of it, which does seem feasible when one considers his girth, but there's something about watching his relentlessness in bearing down to shovel the goop into his mouth, the serving spoon held in his fist in the manner of a toddler, that makes anyone want to avoid proximity to him. This is another reason we regulars keep from the stools directly beside him, and had the wise guy not been with the stripper when he first walked in, I would have told him not to sit beside Hoggin, as I tell most first-timers here. But the wise guy *was* with the stripper, and I didn't want to interfere, and now it strikes me that, had she not had those implants, he wouldn't have wound up caring about Hoggin, and I wonder if this irony sticks in his craw.

Anyway the wise guy isn't exactly in a shits-and-giggles mood after he turns from Hoggin to see the stripper laughing so hard she needs to grab Dorsey's arm to keep from falling off her stool. And it doesn't take long before he, the wise guy, has joined their conversation, or before the stripper's smile has disappeared, and then here's the wise guy and Dorsey talking to the physical exclusion of the stripper, their two faces growing closer, Dorsey raising an index finger to make one of his quasi-valid points, the stripper stepping away from between them and sighing and rolling her eyes, only to notice Hoggin and apparently find the melted ice cream of superior interest, and then the wise guy slides off his stool, now face-to-face with Dorsey, who, since his years in law school, has never avoided an argument. Again, I think to intervene, but maybe, I tell myself, Dorsey will gain oomph from winning this spat; lately the poor sap has been *buried* by what has become of his life.

And this notion, along with the realization that I haven't even sipped from my longneck since Hoggin uncovered this week's vanilla bean smoothie, brings to mind my one obligation of any NFL Sunday: the call to my wife. For years there, Dorsey and I had a good thing going in the sense that we'd convinced our wives, who are friendly with each other because of mutual necessities arising from the bond between Dorsey and me (as well as because both of them are nurses), that there was no payphone in here—*and* that we couldn't use a cell phone because of the steel-reinforced construction of the bar's walls and ceilings. This was one of Dorsey's quasi-valid points, valid in the sense that there is, in fact, no payphone per se, quasi in the sense that there's a phone in the break room any regular can use if he merely drops a quarter in the Kerr jar beside it, but the part about the cell phones was pure bullshit, and because of it Dorsey and I did have a few years in which we, as I mentioned, sowed any wild oats left over from our college days, when we had so much naive faith in our futures we didn't party enough. This late oat-sowing phase is one Dorsey and I no longer discuss, one we now merely serve each other as accomplices for, and it might be a reason we still hang out: As long as we're friends, neither of us will confide in his wife about the particulars of the liberties we took. I'm not saying Dorsey and I were cheating up a storm during that phase; let's just say that, in any sports bar, there will now and again be an emotionally upset, fatigued, middle-aged woman without implants who's found herself in need of a little company in the back seat of her rusted Toyota, and I can't say that Dorsey and I never found ourselves alone in such a back seat with such a woman, the beer in us be damned.

For the record, our inability to use cell phones fell away as an excuse maybe eight years ago, on a Super Bowl Sunday, which, in that particular year, fell smack on Dorsey's twentieth wedding anniversary. Dorsey, after an argument with his wife about how they would celebrate their day, threw what they called a Super Anniversary Party, which consisted of our two families and one regular from here (every regular was invited) watching the game after dinner at his house, the adults among us—Dorsey, his wife, me, mine, and the regular who showed—heading off to catch the fourth quarter here at the bar because a squall knocked out the power on Dorsey's side of town. We'd all drunk enough that none of us considered any downside to leaving Dorsey's place; I myself was blotto enough that, after we arrived here, I played career stud by ordering a Con Ed emergency crew to fix the outage pronto, and, like a dumbshit, I used my cell phone to do it. It wasn't until the next morning that our wives put two and two together to realize we'd been lying to them for years about cell phone feasibility. Needless to say, year twenty-one of Dorsey's marriage wasn't exactly what you'd call bliss.

My wife, though, was more than understanding. It's not that

she went ahead and trusted me, just that she straight-off admitted she loved me more than she could ever love anyone, even the most death-bound patient of hers at her hospital, and that she didn't want to have an argument like the kind we knew Dorsey and his wife would now have for months, so she'd drop the whole subject as long as we'd agree to a deal: She'd drive me here every NFL Sunday at noon, and I'd always call her toward the end of the four o'clock game, so she could drive back over and pick me up. When I agreed to this deal, I thought I was getting off easy—and, for the life of me, didn't get how having her chauffeur me would keep me from the backseat of another woman's car—but the fact is, I haven't had as much as an urge to stray in that manner since we made that deal, no matter how full of barley-pop I've been.

So here I am, calling her on my cell, taking care of my own business rather than attending to Dorsey's with the wise guy, and she answers and, as is our custom, asks how many minutes are left in the game. I tell her four and change, and she makes her usual joke about how one minute of game time equals five minutes of life time, then says she'll be over in half an hour. Then she asks how her Old Man is doing, this nickname for me invented by her after the black December night she was driving me home and I confided in her that sometimes I simply cannot tolerate the process of getting old, and I say OK, and we hang up without good-byes, which is now our way of telling each other everything's all right between us. I'd bet that Dorsey, who I've been watching this whole time, is winning his argument with the wise guy, but the wise guy isn't backing down, and it occurs to me that the wise guy might be armed—and that Dorsey is too drunk to consider this—and now that I've taken care of my own situation, it also occurs to me that if my wife should pass away tonight, say, in a car accident on her way here to prevent me from one of my own, my only friend in the world would be Dorsey, so I make my way toward him and the wise guy, sidling past Hoggin and the stripper to take my stand there. That's what Dorsey calls it, my *taking a stand*: if you ask him, the more years I drink, the more likely I am to find a four-square-foot area in a bar and stand on it with a longneck in my left hand, the thumb of that hand, as I hold the bottle, exactly, he says, an inch and a half from what he guesses is my left nipple, my left elbow two inches farther from my torso than it needs to be. He tells me I have to watch myself because I'm becoming as predictable as Hoggin, that there'll be a day when the regulars will laugh at my taking a stand the way we laugh at Hoggin's ice cream habit, and I have to admit that I think Dorsey has a point, but right now I'm taking my stand beside him while the wise guy is reading him the riot act, so I'm guessing that he, Dorsey, doesn't mind.

Their argument, naturally, has to do with society's rules about the propriety of men interacting with women, about whether a man who's truly a man has the right to touch a woman who is obviously dating another man, and Dorsey is now trying to have it stipulated that it was the *woman* who touched *him*, not the other way around, and also that this is a crucial distinction, one that, according to Dorsey, suggests the wise guy should be discussing the whole matter with the woman and not Dorsey. Then the wise guy tells Dorsey that if he, Dorsey, had a brain, he wouldn't try to tell someone who rules a neighborhood in Brooklyn what to do, and I take these not only as fighting words but as a flat-out warning that the wise guy is in fact packing heat. But Dorsey is either too loaded or too focused on the dig at his intelligence to consider his safety, arguing on about what he calls The Sports Bar Exception, which holds, he says, that *even if it were true* that, *in general*, a man shouldn't talk to a woman obviously dating another man, all bets are off once any man is careless enough to bring a woman into a sports bar. After a pause that suggests the wise guy hasn't followed Dorsey's logic, the wise guy shouts, "You aren't *listening* to me!"—and now a good number of regulars, minus Hoggin (who has downed a third of his ice cream), are glancing away from the Jets to notice that an interpersonal situation has cropped up, and I take my stand closer to the center of the argument, not quite between Dorsey and the wise guy but close enough that my left elbow touches the wise guy's biceps, and I tell Dorsey—who is reexplaining The Sports Bar Exception so slowly I'm about to kick his ass myself—to shut up, which does get the wise guy's attention and finally silence Dorsey. Then I say, as if I'm just making small talk, "You guys know what an alpha male is?"

They both look at me as if I'm more drunk than I am, and both are so thrown by what I've said that they merely sip their drinks, and I go on to tell them a story I've never told before, about the time my wife took in a stray German shepherd. This happened one spring in those years when Dorsey and I had the cell phone excuse going, but I don't mention this tidbit, just lay out what happened, and what happened was my wife felt sorry for this shepherd around the time she also began to feel her change of life, so she babied this shepherd and it took to her, which was fine until the shepherd began sleeping in our bedroom and barking every time my wife and I tried to make love. I also leave out the part about how, because of my age and maybe my long-standing affair with beer in sports bars, attempts at sex were no longer happening all that often between my wife and me, but what I do mention is that I did not at all appreciate the timing of this during-foreplay barking (which I figure gets across the point that no noise, from any dog, helps when it comes to keeping lead in one's pencil), and that I took to throwing shoes at the shepherd to get it to shut its trap, and that this worked, but only to quiet the shepherd, since whenever I'd throw those shoes my wife would get so upset she'd lose interest in our, how can I put it, coitus. Long story short, I end up building a chain link kennel in the side yard for the damned shepherd, who, by the way, is one sizeable motherfucker, but this then causes him to bark out there every night and, for that matter, all night long, and in order to appease both the shepherd and my wife, I rebuild the kennel so it sits flush against our house and leads directly into our kitchen if she opens a small plywood door I cut into the wall after Dorsey swings a variance for a building permit. And this does work to keep the shepherd fairly quiet, though later that winter the sonofabitch gnawed off part of the plywood door and invaded our bedroom one night just after I entered my wife, and nipped my ankle. Of course this pissed me off, but I was also trying to keep my wife happy, so the next day I replaced the plywood door with one I cut from sheet metal, but about three weeks later, the shepherd clawed at the hinges and loosened *that* door enough to interrupt *another* try at coitus, this time springing onto the bed on a dead run, then chomping my wrist.

At this point, to let the wise guy know I'm telling this story more to him than anyone, I show him the scar, but as I do so I dig my left elbow a little harder into him, to make sure he knows, if he hasn't figured it out, that what I'm really doing by telling this story is instructing him to leave the damned bar. Then, with my eyes on him even though the stripper has found her way directly across from me so that she, the wise guy, me, and Dorsey are more or less a tight circle, I tell him what happened next: The shepherd lunged for my wife's throat, and I tackled him, lifted him over my head despite his writhing attempts to bite me, and heaved him at the wall so hard a portrait of our only child fell to the floor. I don't mention that this child was a victim of crib death, just go on to say that the shepherd landed in a tangle and that, for a while there, I thought I'd killed the damned thing, but he ended up fine, whimpering his way out of the room and back out to his kennel, where he's spent every night since in relative peace.

"What was going on," I then say with my eyes still pinned on the wise guy's, "was alpha male competition: the dog thought he was the alpha male, and so did I." Then I ask the wise guy if he now knows what alpha male means, and he nods. "An alpha male's the boss," I say. "And in any given territory," I say, "there can only be one of them." And just after I tell him this, I hold my longneck a little higher, as if toasting to the truth of animal science, and then, without letting my eyes leave his, I patiently drain my beer. Whether he knows I'm bluffing a threat of packed heat of my own is dubious, because we now have one of those standoffs in which no one says anything, but the more time passes, the more I believe I might come out ahead, and at some point all I'm doing is hoping Dorsey continues to keep his mouth shut.

Finally the stripper says, "Did this really happen?"

I hold out my wrist to let her see the scar, my elbow digging harder into the wise guy.

"It was an alpha male thing," I say louder than necessary. "And I'm the alpha male."

Then I simply stand where I am, without moving at all, maybe blinking once or twice. The wise guy finally backs off, and soon Dorsey turns to check out the Jets game, which, I notice, is past the two-minute warning. For a few moments there, it's just the stripper and me, but then the wise guy brings over her sweater and leather jacket and tells me he needs to get her back to Brooklyn, though I ignore him. Mostly I'm thinking about how much I hate how the older you get, the faster your years seem to pass. It should be the other way around, I think as the wise guy pays his bar bill. Or maybe it shouldn't, I think, and the stripper leads him outside.

After the door closes, Dorsey and I watch it to make sure it stays shut, which it does, and then Dorsey faces me and says, "I never heard that story before," and I shrug. He asks how, after all our years of getting in trouble together, I could have nearly killed that dog without telling him so, and I say, "Shit, Dorsey, some things are better kept private."

He glances up at the Jets, then heads off toward the men's room, which leaves me basically alone, so I sit at the bar, two stools away from Hoggin, who puts down his serving spoon, makes sure it's parallel to his half-gallon carton, then says something so loud he can't be mumbling to himself. What he says is: "If there's any alpha male in this place, it's me. And I say you were too mean to that dog."

I think to knock his spongy ass right off his stool, but the urge to do so fails me. After all, my wife is on her way to pick me up, and this reminds me that her freak-of-nature kindness is more than I deserve, and, with that in mind, I set my empty on the bar. Then my forearm is slung around the front of Hoggin's neck, which means there are any number of things I could do to him being the alpha male I am. But all I do is choke him a little. And say: "You know what, Hoggin? You're right."

ACKNOWLEDGMENTS

Jacob M. Appel's "The Appraisal" originally appeared in *New York Stories*.

Porter Fox's "Caribou" originally appeared in *Third Coast*.

James Gish, Jr.'s "Wandering Boy" originally appeared in *Phoebe*.

Dolen Perkins-Valdez's "The Clipping" originally appeared in *Kenyon Review*.

Erin Soros's "Surge" originally appeared in *Iowa Review* and was produced for BBC radio. It appeared in the coordinating anthology, *BBC National Short Story Award* (Short Books).

Mark Wisniewski's "Without Good-byes" originally appeared in the *Southern Review*.

Annie Weatherwax's "The Possibility of Things" originally appeared in *Quarterly West*.

CONTRIBUTORS

Jacob M. Appel has published short fiction in more than eighty literary journals including *Alaska Quarterly Review*, *Greensboro Review*, *Jabberwock Review*, *Southwest Review*, *Southern Indiana Review*, and *Shenandoah*. He is a graduate of Brown University, Harvard Law School, and the Creative Writing Program at New York University. Jacob currently teaches at the Gotham Writers' Workshop in New York City and can also be found at <www.jacobmappel.com>.

Porter Fox writes and teaches in Brooklyn, New York. His fiction and nonfiction have been published in *The New York Times Magazine*, *The Believer*, *Narrative*, *Northwest Review*, and *Third Coast*, among others. He recently completed *Kingdom*, a collection of short stories. For more of his work, see <www.writingofthedisaster.com>.

James Gish, Jr. was born and raised on a small farm in Western Kentucky by parents whose educations stopped after the eighth grade. His life was inexorably shaped in the relentless forge of the Southern Baptist church where it was assumed that he would enter the ministry. He began publishing fiction in college. His wife Jan is a retired computer programmer. His oldest daughter is finishing her Ph.D. at Harvard Divinity School. His youngest daughter is a

Sociology instructor at Sinclair Community College. His greatest influences have been Faulkner, Styron, Eudora Welty and Reynolds Price. He is currently finishing a novel entitled *At The Edge Of Hymns*.

Since publishing his first work, a play, at the age of eighteen, GREGORY LOSELLE has won four Hopwood Awards at The University of Michigan (in Drama, Long Fiction, Poetry and Essay), where he subsequently earned an MFA, as well as The Ruby Lloyd Apsey Award for Playwriting from the University of Alabama, Birmingham. A chapbook, *Phantom Limb*, was published by Pudding House Press last year, and a second chapbook, *Our Parents Dancing*, is forthcoming from the same publisher. A recipient of The Academy of American Poets Prize, he teaches secondary Language Arts and Art History in southeastern Michigan, drilling his students in the distinctions between 'can' and 'may,' 'good' and 'well.'

GERALDINE ANN MARSHALL lives near Paducah, Kentucky with a dachshund dog, Wilbur, and a tuxedo cat, Charlotte, and enjoys families of owls, red-tailed hawks, and bluebirds in the woods surrounding her home. She has two awesome grown daughters, Audrey and Rachel. She has had a novel and several books on natural history and science published. "Secrets of Wood" is from her book in progress, *Learning the Language of Birds: a Charm of Stories of Mothers and Daughters*.

DOLEN PERKINS-VALDEZ has fiction and essays in recent issues of *The Kenyon Review, African American Review, SLI: Studies in Literary Imagination*, and *PMS: PoemMemoirStory*. She is a former waitstaff scholar at Bread Loaf Writers Conference in Vermont. Her debut novel is forthcoming from HarperCollins/Amistad in early 2010. Although she hails from the South, she currently lives in the Pacific Northwest.

MICHAEL SCHIAVONE's fiction has appeared in numerous literary journals and has been recognized by over a dozen award programs.

His debut novel, *Call Me When You Land,* is represented by Barbara Braun Associates, Inc. Along with his wife, son, and four dogs, Michael lives in Gloucester, MA. For more information, please visit <www.michaelschiavone.com>.

Erin Soros has published fiction and non-fiction, most recently in *Indiana Review, The Iowa Review,* and the in-flight magazine *En Route.* Her stories have been produced for the radio by the CBC and BBC as recipients of the CBC Literary Award and the Commonwealth Prize for the short story.

Shubha Venugopal, who holds an MFA in fiction and a PhD in English, teaches literature and writing at the California State University Northridge. She has been a finalist in competitions by *Glimmer Train* and *The Atlantic Monthly,* and her work is anthologized in A Stranger Among Us: Stories of Cross Cultural Collision and Connection. Her stories have appeared in many literary magazines including *Post Road* and *Storyglossia.*

Annie Weatherwax's stories have appeared in *The Southern Review, The Carolina Quarterly, Quarterly West, Calyx, Other Voices,* and others. A graduate of Rhode Island School of Design, she earns a living as a painter and sculptor sculpting superheroes and cartoon characters for Nickelodeon, Disney, Pixar, DC Comics and others. She is currently working on a novel.

Mark Wisniewski is the author of the novel *Confessions of a Polish Used Car Salesman.* His short fiction has won a Pushcart Prize, the 2007 Gival Press Short Story Award, the 2006 Tobias Wolff Award, and the 2006 Texas Institute of Letters Kay Catarulla Award for Best Short Story of 2006; his work has been anthologized in *The Best American Short Stories 2008, The Robert Olen Butler Prize Stories 2007,* and *The Robert Olen Butler Prize Stories 2008.*

DEL SOL PRESS, based out of Washington, D.C., publishes exemplary and edgy fiction, poetry, and nonfiction (mostly contemporary, with the occasional reprint). Founded in 2002, the press sponsors two annual competitions:

THE DEL SOL PRESS POETRY PRIZE is a yearly booklength competition with a January deadline for an unpublished book of poems.

THE ROBERT OLEN BUTLER FICTION PRIZE is awarded for the best short story, published or unpublished. The deadline is in November of each year.

HTTP://WEBDELSOL.COM/DSP

www.ingramcontent.com/pod-product-compliance
Lightning Source LLC
Chambersburg PA
CBHW031127210626
46816CB00015B/1121